Reviews for Dru

-A delightful book full o. .... who welcome you into their world. I'd love to be part of the community evoked in the story, particularly all the ways of working with earth magic and nature. Very much my sort of book- an excellent read!

-I love all books about the Old Ways, love of Nature and the beauty of the Earth. Wonderful narrative, true-to-life characters, mystery and romance, it is all here. Susanna Scott writes with a deft hand and takes the reader on an enchanting journey through a world of lovely people and a creative story. Highly recommend!!

-This book had me in its grip from the first page, it has been a thoroughly wonderful read. I absolutely love how much history is woven into this story.

-Susanna Scott's books are addictive. The characters are so genuine and keep you hooked. I want to live (and eat) in her books! She paints such a clear picture with her words and makes it easy to keep on reading. Her books are a safe and enjoyable place to escape to with all the depressing stuff in the world. Susanna's books are a must-read for anyone who loves nature, animals, and the uplifting power of friendship and community.

-I always enjoy a new book by Susanna Scott and this one has been a joy to read. I love how she has woven together folklore and legend with super characters who you come to know and love during the development of the story.

-This book was an easy enjoyable read, one of those books that you feel invested in the characters and want to know more about them. A book that I know I will want to read again because it made me content. I want to be part of their little community!

Susanna Scott lives in a seaside town on the Yorkshire Coast and enjoys Nature, gardening, Trees – and being with her family.

Also by Susanna Scott
The Gypsy Caravan
The Winterfell Stone
Weaver's Green
Acorn Cottage Christmas
Druid's Oak Farm

*

The Chalk Tower -*A Reverend Grace Danton cosy crime mystery*
(Previously published under the pen-name Sadie Castle)

*

And for children –
Robin Hood and the Wolfshead Tree

Susanna Scott @yorkshirecoastwriter on Facebook

WILDFLOWER WITCH

Susanna Scott

Copyright © Susanna Scott, 2024
All rights reserved.

ISBN: 9798324384319

For my grandparents
Sarah and Frank Barraclough

The word witch derives from the Old English words wicca (male) and wicce (female).
In Old English, the word appeared in two forms: wicca (pronounced something like 'witch-ah'), denoting a man who practises witchcraft or magic, and wicce (pronounced something like 'witch-eh') denoting a woman who practises witchcraft or magic.
oed.com

Prologue

<u>Hilde's Story</u>

Hilde of Farstone looked out of the door of her thatched cottage, onto the patch of ground that she had cultivated into the healthy herb garden she saw now. Around the village, she was now known as the wisewoman of the garden.

Hilde's mother had taught her the art of healing when she was a young girl, living in a settlement in the woods. It had stood her in good stead, as she made her living by the potions and infusions she made from the herbs – and from the healing that was borne out of years of that experience. She could recognize an illness and more often than not, knew what to do to make the person well again. Or the cow. Or the sheep. She wasn't fussy. She just, like her mother and grandmother before her, wanted to help any creature and remove their pain and suffering.

Her mother wouldn't recognize the place now, thought Hilde, turning to look inside her home. The wood they had lived in when she had been alive was mostly cut down and replaced by the few cottages in the small village. Ralph the farmer had wanted his workers to be comfortable and warm, mostly because every winter they were dying off. It was a charitable act, Hilde supposed, even though it was for his own benefit in the end. He had independent wealth on his mother's side so he could afford it.

She missed the trees. There was only a small wood now which she could see from her back door - and she needed to walk in them every day to enjoy the feeling of well-being she gained from them. In the other wood, you could walk for longer and lose yourself.

Her cottage was nearest to the wood and was tucked away at the edge of the village. She was pleased with it, she had to admit. The wood structure was covered in wattle and daub and she was warmer in winter than she had ever been. As she was a widow, she held tenement for life as long as she didn't marry again, which she wouldn't. Then she could pass it on to her daughter as this house was much better than the travelling life Agnes was living at the moment – she would be glad of it eventually.

She crossed the floor of beaten earth covered in rushes and went over to the small cauldron heating over the fire. She stirred the contents and put the spoon to her lips. Removing it from the just-glowing fire, she waited for it to cool before decanting some into the small vial. She would take it up to Farmer Ralph's to give to his young daughter, along with one of her special earthenware pots containing goose fat mixed with powdered mustard seeds, to rub on her chest. The girl tended towards coughs and colds and this would help to stave off any further congestion. Along with honey from her father's bees at the farm, in hot water before bedtime.

Hilde wanted to keep on his good side as she had a favour to ask him. She walked past the herbs drying from the wooden beams, past the trestle table where she mixed and ground the potions and poultices, until she stood on the threshold.

She looked past her herbs and out to the small wood. Between the two was an area of grassland that had never been used for grazing, although her chickens wandered onto it all the time. She wanted to ask Ralph if she could use it to plant more herbs and flowers to use for her healing. In exchange, she could promise to let him have his remedies for free. He was a good man, so Hilde thought he might give her the land as it was of no use to him. Ralph was very interested in the art of healing and often asked her questions about her remedies.

Hilde collected her vial and the pot containing her salve, then set off to call for Meg, her neighbour, who was taking some chicken broth for the girl. Between them, they would cure her. She hoped that Ralph would be grateful enough to look kindly on her entreaty, regarding the meadow behind her cottage.

Chapter 1

Gallipot Cottage, in the village of Farstone, appeared at first glance to be uncared for and unloved. The windows were old-fashioned tiny-paned windows, each wooden surround in bad need of a coat of paint. The guttering was hanging off at one end and weeds were growing thickly along the narrow 17th-century bricks as they met the pavement. And Flora absolutely *loved* it on sight!

She had wished for character – and here she had it in spades. With not having a photo or even a Google street view as it was half-hidden around a corner, her thoughts had run wild and imagined a seventies big-windowed shop tacked onto a dark forbidding Victorian-looking cottage. Even though she knew it was decades older. Her imagination was a weird and wonderful thing.

Where other people would call it dilapidated, she would call it characterful. Where other people would see an ocean of work, she saw an opportunity to make it her own. The big window to the right, she supposed was the shop. It had a 'Ye Olde Tucke Shoppe' vibe about it that she liked, never 'minde' that a few of the 'smalle' panes were cracked… It even had a couple of 'Bull's Eye' panes too, which was an indication of its age.

She walked up to this window and peered in, hoping to see stray tins of Borthwick's Baking Powder, old packets of Lyon's tea and the odd jar of sticky barley sugar twists left there. Instead, she saw a few dead and desiccated spider bodies- one which could have been the original model for Aragog – and a few big, dusty moth corpses. She couldn't see anything else as yellowing newspaper was pinned against the glass. Not exactly showing reports of the Titanic disaster but hardly up to date either.

Flora stepped back for a better look at her new home, Gallipot Cottage. She had looked up the strange name and it was apparently a special earthenware pot that apothecaries and medical people used to put their creams and balms in. Which, when she thought about it, was absolutely perfect for her. She wondered what Great Aunt Sybil had used the shop for, before she became too old and had to give it up.

She wasn't her real great aunt, only an old friend of her parents as far as she could make out. After the initial interest that Flora had shown in the strangely dressed old person who visited when she was seven, neither she nor her mum and dad had mentioned her again. Which is why it was such a shock, her being left this place. Why would she do that? Flora supposed she had no one else to leave it to and, taking in the whole building now, she sent a promise to wherever Sybil had passed on to, that she would look after the place for her.

She checked her watch, the gold one that was her mother's, then turned to look around her. From here she could see down the village street to her right. There was a sign on the corner opposite her, pointing down there to Peverel Hall. She could also see the swinging sign of an old, low pub but nothing or no one else could be seen. Stepping to her right a little as she was tucked away in a corner at the edge of the village, she could now see the road she'd driven in on, set almost at right angles to the one she stood on.

This curved street was called High Street. It must have taxed the street planner's inventive processes to come up with that one. Although, peering closer, the street in front of her was High Street North and the one that curved to her right, was High Street East. Nowhere on either of these High Street combinations was an old woman, possibly on a Zimmer frame, to be seen. Not even a Hell's Granny on a souped-up mobility scooter, on course to run over her toes at 25 miles per hour. She had seen a couple of people on her way up, both middle-aged and not likely to be Sybil's best friend - the one she was supposed to be meeting fifteen minutes ago. The one who had the keys to the cottage. Why on earth hadn't the solicitor given Flora her address?

There was a noise somewhere to her left - down High Street North. It came from a small shop as a woman stepped out and closed the door behind her. Flora started to walk towards her expectantly but she got into a car and drove off.

If the shop was open, she could ask there if anyone knew of a Margaret Harker, Sybil Gardwicke's friend. She locked the door of the car that contained many of her worldly possessions and which she had pulled onto the convenient grass patch at the side of the cottage.

Opening the shop door, she saw rows and rows of wooden shelves. Oh, joy of joys, she thought, a bookshop! Mostly second-hand books by the look of it although there was a table nearby, promoting local authors. There were also a few small round tables, each with a couple of chairs, positioned in the window. At the furthest one sat an elderly woman, simultaneously drinking coffee and avidly reading a book held up in front of her. Flora didn't think she had noticed her come in. Possibly not Margaret?

A man was standing at a small wooden counter to the left of the author table. He had a plumpish, kind face with laughter lines around his eyes. His hair was a faded red and it stuck up on end as though he had run his hand through it.

'Can I help you? You look a bit lost' he smiled.

'I'm looking for someone but I'm delighted to have found a bookshop here' she smiled back. 'I'm sure I'll be a regular visitor. I was supposed to meet this lady, a Margaret Harker?'

'Margaret Ha–, Oh, Peggy? I haven't seen her around today but I'm sure Jen will be able to show you where she lives' he suddenly looked suspicious, 'Are you a friend?'

'I've never met her but she was a friend of my great aunt and I was supposed to be meeting her over fifteen minutes ago.'

'That's okay then. She's quite a private person so…' He stuck his head through a doorway and shouted. 'Jen, can you come down here a minute?'

There were light footsteps on the stairs and a woman in her thirties emerged. Her hair was nearly as dark as Flora's but was cut shorter, coming to just below her shoulders. It was pushed behind her ears to reveal huge, dangling gold earrings in a complicated knot pattern.

Flora was so fascinated by them that she didn't register the woman's abrupt halt and when she did, her eyebrows drew together in confusion. The woman was staring at her in what looked like horror – open-mouthed and wide-eyed – with all her features frozen in shock.

Flora tore her gaze away to send a mute appeal to the man who, with a worried frown, spoke to the woman.

'Jen…?'

Flora turned towards the woman who was still frozen. Then suddenly and with an obvious effort, the woman turned and ran back up the stairs, leaving the man staring at Flora in embarrassment.

'I'm sorry. I don't know– She never–' he collected himself together. 'My name's Steve Cayley, Jen's husband.'

He put his head down as, he held his hand out, as though this fact wouldn't commend him to anyone at the moment.

'I'll show you where Peggy lives?'

He moved towards the doorway and started to point further down High Street East, a couple of cottages past Flora's, when he stood up straight.

'Oh, there she is.'

Flora leaned forward in the direction he now indicated and saw a woman standing outside Gallipot Cottage with her arms folded, looking for all the world as if she'd been waiting there for hours.

Flora lifted her eyes to heaven, gave her thanks to Steve and ran out of the shop.

'I was here earlier' Why was she apologizing? 'but I couldn't see anyone so I thought I'd go to the shop to ask.'

She finished this speech whilst Margaret – Peggy – regarded her calmly, not changing the expression in her open face. She continued to do this for what seemed like minutes and Flora was starting to feel very uncomfortable, like she was being dissected by secret laser beams shooting from Peggy's eyes. In fact, she was starting to feel uncomfortable – not just with the reactions of the two women this morning – but with the whole idea of moving to this village.

She had been so excited when she heard she had inherited the shop and cottage from her 'Great Aunt' Sybil. She also felt guilty because if she had known of the bond that Sybil obviously felt with her, she would have made an effort to see her. She had been consigned to childhood memories and hadn't emerged until a couple of months ago. She had been in the process of selling her parent's house, both now sadly deceased, to get somewhere smaller without a mortgage. This had come at the perfect time as she could use the money, after she'd paid the old mortgage off, to do this place up.

She had always wanted to live in the country rather than the busy town she had been brought up in, especially here in Yorkshire which she had always felt an affinity with, so it was a dream come true. Or had been until everyone started behaving like she'd dropped into a dark folk story where the womenfolk sacrifice newcomers to the Green Man of the forest if they don't like the look of them. She glanced at her car and wondered how quickly she could sprint there.

'I knew you must be here; your car is parked at the side.'

Peggy stated this laconically and with impeccable logic. Flora attempted a smile and received what might have been a smile in return. The corners of Peggy's mouth lifted slightly and her eyes crinkled a little more than they already were but she had one of those immobile faces that gave nothing away unless they wanted to. Flora wasn't sure she would manage to pick her out of a police line-up.

Yet somehow, the old woman seemed to give forth a quiet serenity which now put Flora at her ease. One thing which would make her stand out in a line-up was the halo of frizzy, white, curly hair which surrounded her face, incongruously topped off with an orange woolly hat.

'Here's the keys' Peggy stated, bringing Flora out of her reverie. 'Don't know as how you'll be able to stay in this place tonight. Hasn't been lived in for a few months. Let's have a look and see.'

Peggy put the keys in the younger woman's outstretched hand and walked slowly round to the right side of the cottage. Flora's car was parked in front of a high laurel hedge with a tall gate at the cottage end of it. It obscured the view behind it but just before that was a side door, wooden with paint flaking off. Peggy nodded towards it and Flora placed the key in the lock with a mixture of excitement and dread.

Chapter 2

They entered straight into the kitchen. It was big and old-fashioned with an ancient range oven of indeterminate make along the left-hand wall. In the centre was an old wooden table scrubbed almost white with use over many years. On the wall to her right was a big, butler sink with a large window above it, with more of the tiny panes. On the same wall was a doorway leading outside and there was a solid wood dresser further along. In the far corner was a small round table with two chairs and, above it, another smaller window overlooking the back of the house.

Immediately, Flora's mind started whirring into action. She spoke her thoughts out loud.

'I wonder if I'd be allowed to put French doors in or even a sliding door, straight out from that table and onto a patio? If there isn't a patio,

I'll make one. I'll spend a lot of time in that corner then.'

She whipped her head round to look at Peggy, expecting disapproval at new ideas. What she got was a beaming smile which completely threw her. The smile lit up Peggy's face, making her cheeks look like rosy apples and making her hooded eyes almost disappear with happiness. What a transformation! Flora could hardly believe it.

'I'm sorry' she went on in her original frame of mind, 'it must seem as though I'm coming into your friend's house and immediately taking it over.'

Peggy shook her head.

'What it seems as though you're doing, is making plans to live here. Is that right? We thought you might be going to sell it.'

'I wouldn't dream of selling it.' Flora looked horrified. 'I'm so looking forward to living here and making it my own. I'm going to get the shop restored too.'

The older woman nodded her head slowly, still looking very pleased. Flora saw a thought flutter across her face, animating it again. She pointed through a door next to the range which led to a short hallway.

'Let me show you the shop. It's in a worse state than the house because your…Sybil lived in the house till her death but stopped using the shop at least five years ago. I don't think it will take much to get it going again.'

She followed her down the passage, through a door on her left and into the shop. There wasn't anything there to speak of. They had emerged through the door and straight behind a lovely old wooden counter, similar to the one in the bookshop. Beyond that, there were a few empty shelves, a tiled floor with a sweeping brush abandoned across it and a deep windowsill at this side of the newspaper-covered windows. All of this was littered with the bodies of dead insects and, more worryingly, what looked like a decomposed mouse in the corner.

There were a couple of random plastic chairs at the other side of the counter, looking incongruous in a shop that could otherwise have come out of Dickens. There was a door in the left-hand wall which she thought was a cupboard but upon investigation was a small room with a frosted window, which must have been the small window looking out over the driveway, just before the kitchen door. She thought it had been a scullery as there were a couple of stone shelves in it with a rickety wooden table at the far end. Back in the shop, a door to the left of the window led straight out onto the street. Perfect.

'It's not too bad. It's all I'll really want inside fitment-wise apart from more shelves and perhaps a glass front to the counter. I can make a great display on the windowsill. A lick of paint to brighten it up – and I'll need to scrub the terracotta tiles and mend the window frames before I paint them. I'm not going to paint the wood of the counter...'

She looked at Peggy in case she thought she was going to destroy the character,

'Only the walls and window frames. This wood I'll polish up with beeswax. It will look beautiful.'

She was treated to another of Peggy's smiles and again got the impression that they were only reserved for special occasions.

'I'd like to know more about Sybil when you have the time if that's alright with you?'

This was Sybil's oldest friend and she reasoned that she would know more about her elusive benefactress than anyone else. The solicitor didn't even know much about her – or wasn't saying – and her parents couldn't have known much as they never mentioned her.

'I'd like that. Sometime after you're settled in, maybe?'

Peggy spoke with a Yorkshire 'burr' but with slightly different inflections from any other Yorkshire dialect she had heard before. She had heard about insular, isolated villages like this would have been until less than a century ago, where the speech sounded almost like a foreign language. This was recognisable – but with a hint of 'difference'. She turned to Flora now.

'What were you going to sell in the shop?'

She asked this in a hesitant manner as though dreading the answer would be 'Farstone souvenir key rings and postcards' or even 'blow-up rubber dolls'.

'Natural Healing' she replied, putting Peggy out of her misery, although Peggy's face animated itself for a few seconds to a shocked expression. Flora attempted to explain.

'It's alright, I have a degree in Herbal medicine, approved by the National Institute of Medical Herbalists. I didn't want to do this as I feel that healing with herbs should be instinctive but you need one to be able to practice legally. In case you poison someone accidentally I suppose, so I can see their point.'

No reaction from Peggy who just stared at her. She felt a need to qualify her decision.

'It would only be for mild illnesses, I wouldn't interfere with more serious things where I knew I wouldn't be able to help, I'd send them to a doctor. Doctor's appointments are so difficult to get nowadays that I could alleviate some of the suffering while they waited.'

Still no reaction but the stare was more intense.

'I can see now I've arrived here that I wouldn't get passing trade' she stammered, feeling sweat breaking out on her forehead under the woman's gaze, 'but you get walkers here – and it's a pretty place to make a special journey to. And then there's the local people who are just as important to me. And I intend to do an online version of my shop with dried ingredients like culinary herbs to promote health - and herbal teas for wellbeing and promoting sleep – and, and…herb sachets and pillows -because I can't sell medicine online…'

Flora was aware she was babbling now. She looked at Peggy as a mouse would at a hovering kestrel. She seemed to be on the verge of speaking.

'Did you *know* what this shop was before?' she eventually asked Flora.

'N – no. Only that it was a shop some years previously. Sweetshop?' she tried, thinking of the bull's eye windows.

'I will tell you the whole story when you are settled in and know our ways but, Sybil was a healer. This wasn't as much a shop as a consulting room.'

Flora's eyes opened wide in amazement. Her parents had never mentioned this and neither had Sybil on the one occasion that she had met her in her parents' garden. She remembered her parents being annoyed at Sybil asking her questions but Flora had been quite happy to answer them. She had quite liked the old woman, even if she dressed a little strangely.

'I had no idea' Flora spoke in a reverent whisper as though respecting her memory. 'That could be why I felt an affinity with her when I was a child. It's very strange. Almost like a message being passed down through the ages' Flora lifted her eyes to look at Peggy, whose own eyes glistened.

'A twist of fate?' Peggy muttered to herself before addressing Flora.

'Will you buy the things in that you need? The herbs? In plastic packets and plastic bottles?' she spat dismissively. Flora smiled.

'No, I want to grow them myself. I mean, I might have to buy some in from other natural sources until I get the plants established. The solicitor says there's a garden with the house and I'm hoping it will be big enough to grow what I need.'

There was a sound from Peggy, somewhere between a wheeze and a laugh. Then she sighed and her eyes crinkled in what Flora was beginning to recognise as quiet humour.

'Follow me' was all she said.

So Flora followed her out of the shop, back down the passage and through to the kitchen. Picking the keys up from the kitchen table, she unlocked the back door and threw it open.

At first, Flora couldn't take in what she was seeing. There was a profusion of colour, as though a large Monet print had been spread out before her.

Slowly, she stepped out onto the patio and focused on the land beyond it. Not just a garden. Not just a small patch of land to grow herbs - but a whole meadow. Yet she didn't have to grow healing herbs now because the meadow in front of her was full of them. Every conceivable kind of wildflower waved their heads around in the gentle breeze. A riot of colour with bees and other insects flying from bloom to bloom. Her own, her very own, wildflower meadow.

A laugh burst from Flora and she couldn't be sure but it sounded like Peggy had joined in. Flora clapped her hands and then immediately put them to her eyes as she could feel the happy tears starting to flow.

Chapter 3

A smile came to Flora's lips as she remembered her emotional reaction to the wildflowers. She had come out of a dream to see Peggy beaming her special smile in her direction.

'Is it really all mine? Even the little wood that runs on from the meadow?' she breathed.

'It is' replied Peggy with a satisfied air. 'One of your – of Sybil's ancestors got the land and wood, Pookey Wood it's called, from the local farmer. Later, when the farmer's descendant was ennobled, becoming Sir Ralph Peverel for services rendered during the civil war, he signed the deeds of this cottage and its land, over to all descendants of the Gardwickes.'

'I'm not a Gardwicke, I'm a Goode' frowned Flora.

'To all intents and purposes, you are a Gardwicke. This is your cottage, no doubt about it. Signed over to you by Miss Sybil Gardwicke herself.'

As Peggy stepped out onto the driveway, she nodded towards Flora.

'I wasn't sure if this Flora Goode was going to be the sort of person to appreciate her inheritance and what it means – but I can see now that you are. It can't be a coincidence that your life was set on the same course as Sybil's long before you knew anything about her or this cottage. It is fate. I knew from the moment you mentioned Natural Healing that you were the right one.'

*

Looking back now, that would have explained the reticence, the wariness on the other woman's part at first. She didn't want her friend's legacy to be covered in concrete and trampolines. There was no chance of that. This wildflower meadow was something she could only have dreamt of. Her original plans had been to replicate this in miniature - she counted herbs and wildflowers as the same thing, they could almost all cure, soothe or heal all ills – and sometimes make you ill or even kill, if you didn't know your plants. Luckily, she did. Now she didn't have to plant anything. Sybil had done it already, as if to Flora's own specifications.

When she had thought of planting her herb garden, she thought of a fairly small garden, not land. And to have the wood as well. That wasn't for planting, apart from the flowers that grew best in shade and they would probably grow naturally there. No, she wanted it to walk in, to breathe the air, smell the trees, enjoy their shade. She wanted to be able to hug and talk to them if she wanted. In her frequent trips to the forest near her hometown, there had always been others around. Lots of them. The grown-ups would probably have carted their children off to safety if they'd come across her hugging a beech tree or having an intense conversation with a sycamore. Mind you, she'd probably have got more sense out of the sycamore than she'd have got out of most of her friends.

They weren't bad people, her friends, they just wanted nightclubs, drinking, loud music and lots and lots of men. And she…didn't.

The will had been written just after Sybil's visit to see her, just over seventeen years ago. It was lodged with her solicitor, not just until Sybil's death but of her parents, Bill and Hester

Goode's deaths, if Sybil should predecease them. In the event, they had died five and three years ago respectively. Flora had puzzled over this stipulation but when she asked the solicitor, he just shrugged and said that Sybil Gardwicke was known to be mildly eccentric. This only made Flora wish she'd known her, at least for the last three years when she didn't have any family whatsoever and even a fake great aunt would have been better than being an 'abandoned orphan'.

Her parents had been well into their forties when they'd had her – 'a late blessing from God' they said, although they were never particularly religious. She hadn't expected to lose them quite so soon.

Sighing and changing her train of thought, she looked out at the meadow and thought how alike she and Sybil must have been considering they were not relatives and the title of Great Aunt, according to her mother was one of respect. There was an awful lot to ask Peggy. What was that she'd said as she left? It was fate? Flora was 'the right one'? What did that mean?

*

She examined the rest of the house after Peggy had left. She was pleasantly surprised at its condition. There was the most perfect little sitting room at the other side of the passage, looking out to the front. It was just big enough for her – and her alone. After a couple of failed relationships – alone was what she wanted. It had an old brick fireplace in the same narrow, handmade bricks the cottage was made from. There was an open fire with a dog grate. At either side was a thick stone pillar with some carvings on it which looked as old as the stone itself. Possibly limestone, being Yorkshire but that was just a guess. One of the carvings looked familiar and she was surprised to see it was very similar to the odd bookshop woman's dangly earrings.

Through the tiny-squared glass window, she could make out the bow window of the bookshop. She was looking forward to going to restock her books, as long as the strange woman didn't run off every time she took some books up to the counter. Her husband seemed nice at least.

Sybil's furnishings were still in place. Instead of finding this a bit spooky, she felt somehow comforted by it. There was a small desk underneath the window and a beautifully simple, carved wooden chair pushed underneath it. A pot with pens in was standing on it, with a bottle of black ink next to it. There was an old comfortable–looking armchair next to the fire with a brightly-coloured, knitted throw over the back of it.

To the left of the chair was a round wooden table and on the far wall stood an old squashy red sofa. An Axminster-style rug stood in the centre of the polished floorboards surrounding it. There was a bookcase in the far corner to the left of the fire with all the books still there. It all combined to make Flora feel that Sybil had just walked out to go to the grocers and would be back any moment.

There were two and a half bedrooms at the top of a winding wooden staircase. One was a smaller empty one to the front which she would appropriate as an office for the business she hoped to have. There was a box room next to it, used as a storage space, which would be handy. However, at this precise moment, she didn't have a lot to store. Then there was the bedroom at the back which she had picked as hers. It was obviously Sybil's too as there was an old metal bed frame in the centre of the right-hand wall and an old, honey-coloured wooden chest of drawers against the other wall. A small high wicker table stood next to the bed, a reading lamp still in place.

The whole cottage was much lighter than she thought it would be, but because it had been empty for so long, it needed a good airing before she could move in. She decided she would just buy a new mattress for this bed frame as it rather appealed to her sense of history. Flora would wait to talk to Peggy until she had found a room for a couple of days. The old woman hadn't invited her to stay at her place, but to be honest, she didn't really look the sociable type. She had melted a little though when she realised Flora had the same aims as Sybil. It seemed like she had been marked 'Approved'.

The Peverel Arms had rooms advertised on the internet. It was a walker's paradise around here and therefore a walker's pub. It was to be hoped the said walkers hadn't booked all the rooms up before she could get there. She locked the back door whilst memorising the meadow then went to leave the kitchen by the side door.

'Oh, what are you doing here?'

She bent down to stroke a small black cat with a white streak behind its ear, that made a beeline for her and rubbed around her ankles. She wondered briefly if she'd inherited a cat from Sybil too but dismissed it. It only looked like a young cat, could it have come in here with Peggy?

'Whatever' she said to the cat, 'you can't stay here. I'm locking up.'

She shooed it outside and was treated to a very disdainful look.

Chapter 4

After parking her car in the pub car park, Flora went into the lounge and asked the young girl behind the bar if they had a room for the night. It took the girl, Mary, around fifteen minutes to say yes. On the way, she explained 'how busy they had been over Easter with the walkers but it always tails off and then gets busy again a short while later but because this was just after Easter they had a nice room at the front if she wanted it and she'd be happy to show her it if she'd just like to look at the menu if she wanted a meal and then she could get her order in but she didn't have to it was all right in fact I can show you up there first now if you just let me check...'

Even though Mary didn't appear to have taken a breath during this whole monologue, she still had the energy to run through to a room at the back before popping her head back around to say,

'I'm sorry. I know I talk too much. My dad's always telling me off over it and I keep saying I'll stop and well anyway. I'll just–' and she flew into the back room again.

A woman came out shaking her head and laughing which Flora thought was a sort of apology.

'She lets her mouth run away with her when she's nervous. She'll be better when she gets to know you. Flora Goode? You have Sybil's cottage now?'

The woman, Mary's mother from the looks of her, was a nice plumpish woman with a ruddy face and hair the colour of straw. She told Mary to watch the bar while she showed Flora up to a room. It was a pleasant, light room overlooking the street. She would eat in the bar but put in an order for later and see what she could find out from Peggy first.

In the bar she found the menu and ordered the chicken and vegetable homemade pie for an hour's time, to be safe. A woman stood further down the bar. She was rather elegant but appeared to have a small knitting needle stuck in her silver hair which was swept up off her face.

She introduced herself in a very plummy voice and asked if Flora wanted to join her in a gin. Flora didn't as she was going out but she did appreciate the gesture, even though the woman - who had a strange name she'd already forgotten - was looking at her with obvious curiosity. After exchanging another few words with her, the woman drank up and went out of the door, passing an old man leaning against the door jamb. He seemed to be staring at Flora but it was hard to tell as his hood was pulled down, almost covering his face, apart from two pinpricks of light shining through, indicating where his eyes were.

Flora pulled on her coat to go to Peggy's and as she made for the door, the old man made a mock bow towards her and walked over to the bar like a much younger man. It was probably his clothes that made him seem older. A khaki greatcoat almost in rags and underneath, a hooded top that was once green but now had faded to match the coat. He made her feel uncomfortable. She wondered if it was because he was what she would call a tramp, although they probably had a more PC name today. Not homeless as such but a soul, perhaps damaged, who wandered from place to place.

Now, when she got outside she could see why he'd been wearing the hood. It had started drizzling. She pulled the grey, full-length raincoat around her and put the hood up, making for where Peggy had said she lived, just down from Gallipot Cottage. After knocking for a few minutes on both the front and the back doors she made her way to the inn again. It would wait until tomorrow.

As she crossed the road she could see the sign for Peverel Hall and decided to have a quick look. The driveway curved round through tall trees and she could see the corner of a honey-coloured building through the branches. As the Peverel Hall sign had a smaller 'Private' written underneath, she thought she'd better not chance her luck.

When she turned back, she caught sight of a narrow lane by the side of the last cottage, across the road. This one didn't appear to have a Private sign on display and as she could glimpse some moorland beyond, she decided that would do instead to feed her curiosity.

She walked up the little lane, which seemed like it was a public bridleway, judging by the hoof marks left in the soft earth. She was on the moors almost immediately. The village was remote and probably difficult to reach in bad, winter weather. To reach it earlier, she had to negotiate a good few miles of hairpin bends on tiny, narrow lanes with steep drops at one side as she drove. She wasn't a nervous driver but she dreaded meeting anyone coming the other way. As this was the only way in or out of the village, she gritted her teeth and got on with it. She expected she would become used to it in time.

This village was a little oasis in the middle of miles and miles of moorland. The guidebook mentioned it had grown up around a farm, which was now Peverel Hall. The farm kept sheep for their wool and to a lesser degree for their meat. It had produced honey too and there were crops grown in the fertile soil which lay in the open vale below the moors. The place was self-sufficient in the Middle Ages and over the years, modern shops had been added to make it much the same now.

There was a baker, a hardware shop, a butcher and a mini-market selling fresh produce. There was also a combined newsagents and post office and she remembered passing tea rooms on her way in. There was the Peverel Arms, which sported a few wooden benches on a patch of green in front of it, waiting for good weather.

And, it seemed, there was a bookshop which doubled as a coffee shop. Flora would look forward to going in there again if she only saw the man instead of the odd woman.

She strode out, pulling her hood tightly around her face. It was still only drizzling but her hair had a tendency to go frizzy in the damp. It was slightly misty at ground level, hovering above the peat. Turning around as she reached the top of a gently sloping hill, she saw the village in all its glory, in the setting it had inhabited comfortably for hundreds of years.

She wanted to find out more about Farstone now she had arrived. Trying to recall its history, she remembered it had been described as an ancient village. It was known as a village from Anglo-Saxon times but Neolithic implements had been found in a dig at Peverel Hall, indicating a much older settlement.

Farstone nestled down there, hardly much bigger than it would have been in those far-off days. New housing developments wouldn't occur here as there were no jobs for young families. What had the solicitor said? There were mostly the same families - the same names, as there always had been.

This stirred a memory of something else in the guidebook. The tradition of folklore in Farstone was strong. Everything from witches and spectral hounds to fairies and goblins was supposed to put in a regular appearance here, according to legend. Flora supposed they had nothing much else to do in the long winter months of yesteryear than sit around and tell these stories.

She gradually became aware of a pounding of the earth somewhere behind her. She spun around and saw a horse and rider about a hundred yards away about to cross her path. She felt that she was seeing a rerun of a gothic horror film and wondered briefly if the rider was headless.

The man was galloping at full speed along a moorland track on a coal-black horse. The rider's hair was blown into a wild black halo and the mane of the horse streamed behind its magnificent, proud head. A huge animal, some sort of dog perhaps, followed them. She couldn't help but stare and was shocked when suddenly the figure noticed her and abruptly pulled his steed up short, causing the animal to rear up. The rider turned in his saddle and stared at Flora for long minutes before turning along another track, leading further out onto the moor.

She rubbed her eyes as if to dispel any mirage that had appeared in front of her or hallucination caused by tiredness. It must have worked because when she looked up again, the horseman had disappeared.

Chapter 5

Farstone village, in the middle of Farstone Moor, had been improved and updated in the late 17th century. Before that, it was a cluster of buildings that had sprung up in a wood that surrounded the farm in Saxon times. It was then improved by Ralph the farmer into wattle and daub constructions, more weatherproof than the rough huts they had before. They were independent from Ralph's farm but they relied on it for their wages. They helped each other out, the farm owners being unusual in that they were good to their workers. They weren't particularly well off to start with and relied on the houses nearby for their help.

When a descendant, also Ralph and now named Peverel, came into money in the 1600s, he not only built himself a grand house in place of the small farmhouse, but he improved or rebuilt all the workers' houses too. He called his grand house Peverel Hall. The village was known as Farstone after the moor that surrounded it. Farstone was derived from Fairystone or Faestone, from the folklore legend that the moor was still inhabited by the Fae, as it had been long before humans made their home in these parts.

It was to Peverel Hall that Peggy Harker now made her way, missing Flora's visit to her cottage by at least ten minutes. This was the home of the present Ralph Peverel, now a Sir after his ancestors were ennobled by Charles II, as were most of those in charge who fought on his or his father's side in the Civil War. The current Sir Ralph was away from home as usual. At the moment he was supervising the building of houses for families in need in Africa. The desire to help people had never left the family and consequently he wasn't in the village he loved as much as he wanted to be. It was also said that he was running away from something in his past.

His older sister, Binky - Bianca was her given name after a Spanish godmother - ran the place most of the time, although the farm itself had been sold off, just leaving the Hall and extensive grounds. Binky was mostly a lady of leisure since she retired from the acting profession last year, fed up with being relegated to second-rate pantos in out-of-the-way places. Being middle-aged in the acting profession wasn't much fun, although even Binky's closest friends couldn't say she was ever a *good* actress, even when she was young.

Peggy rang the ornate doorbell at the front of the Hall. Chilvers the old retainer who used to be Binky's nanny and was therefore ancient, took a while to answer. The door creaked open.

'She's up at t'Folly with t'other'un' she announced before shutting the door again.

Peggy grinned to herself and set off for the Folly, a few minutes' walk away. It was in a sunny corner of the grounds but still well hidden from the house by the grove of horse chestnut trees surrounding three sides. A tree-lined path led directly to it.

Standing in the late afternoon sun, the Folly looked magnificent. It was erected when the original Hall was built by the newly ennobled Gentleman farmer. Peggy surveyed it again with pleasure, even though she had known it all her life. It had been made to represent an old castle ruin or perhaps a temple. A wall at the left-hand side seemed as though it had belonged to another structure but had crumbled away with age. A tree seemed to be growing through the wall as if propping the remaining wall up. On the right side was a much smaller wall with ivy growing over the top, which looked like the remains of a much taller boundary wall. These were all illusions, as it had been built that way to represent a fairy tale ruin in the first place. Inside the ancient-looking stone, mellowed with age and covered with climbing plants as though being reclaimed by nature, was a perfectly serviceable large room. The walls were plastered, the ceiling was high and it had always been used as a meeting place - or a dining place for generations of Peverels to have their teas and indoor picnics. It was almost al fresco on hot summer days when the large doors, with their floor-to-ceiling windows, were thrown open to the elements.

At the dining table now were seated two women. One was fairly young and attractive with her dark hair pushed behind her ears. She was wearing a mutinous expression. The other, much older but still younger than Peggy by over twenty years, wore her permanent surprised look and her habitual smiley face. Her hair was silver and piled onto her head in a messy style which was kept in place by what looked like a large Neolithic bone hairpin.

The sun was disappearing to be replaced by a fine drizzle, so Peggy hurried in.

'Merry meet' said Peggy as she climbed the steps.

'Merry meet' replied Binky Peverel, whilst the younger woman settled for a glowering silence.

'What's with the face?' asked Peggy in her customary direct manner.

'What do you think? 'replied Jen Cayley in like manner and before Peggy could answer, she told her anyway.

'She turned up in our shop earlier and you didn't give me any warning. Steve called me through to speak to her and - my God - I *couldn't* speak. I had to run out. She is the spitting image of my sister Matty. How do you think I *felt*?'

The older woman sat herself down and fixed Jen with her hooded eyes before speaking calmly.

'You knew she was coming here, Jennet. I even told you the date she was taking possession of Sybil's cottage. What I couldn't tell you was how much Flora looks like her mother. Her real mother. I hadn't seen her at all. Remember Sybil had only seen her once and was banned from seeing her again after that time, for the child's sake, so they said. To give her a 'normal' upbringing. Sybil knew she had made the decision that led to this so she felt, on her honour, that she had no choice. I was shocked myself at the likeness when I saw her so I can imagine what it must have felt like for you. I'm sorry for what you went through but you can't blame me.'

Jen lowered her eyes and had the grace to look ashamed.

'And she knows nothing?' she eventually asked.

Peggy shook her head.

'But surely–'

'I saw her in the Peverel Arms not half an hour ago' Binky cut in 'and yes, the likeness to Matilda was very obvious. I introduced myself and welcomed her to the village which is a good job as you two seem to have done nothing but gawp at the poor girl, like the village idiots she probably takes us for. She seemed very nice.'

'She did' agreed Peggy 'and she asked to come round to find out more about her Great Aunt Sybil. She said Great Aunt in invisible inverted commas as she doesn't believe her to be her real great aunt. Which of course she was.'

'Does she have any powers?'

'Now how am I to know that on such short acquaintance, Jennet?'

'Well, she needs to be told of her ancestry. About the village. But more to the point, she needs to know who her real mother was.'

'Then she'll know you're her aunt. Will that sit well with you?'

'I suppose it will have to.' Jen replied unsurely ' but this is something Sybil should have done.'

'Firstly, don't forget the girl has no idea of any of this.'

'I'm in two minds whether she just ought to be left in peace. It's a lot to surprise one person with – and there's no guarantee that she'll take it well.'

'Binky!' said Jen, outraged.

'I have a feeling she will take it as calmly as is possible' said Peggy, 'She doesn't seem the sort to throw hissy fits or go into a deep decline. Anyway, no doubt Sybil would have told her if she had contact with her but she promised Bill and Hester on Flora's life when the child was 7 years old. Sybil had made the handing over when she was a baby – had chosen the parents, so it was understood. Why Sybil broke her promise in the first place was that she needed to know at the First Age if there was anything in the child - but she wouldn't break that promise again.'

'Was that because she found a power?' Jen asked.

'Apparently so.'

There was an intake of breath from the others.

'So there's nothing we can do to let her know the circumstances of her birth or what sort of a village she was born into?'

Peggy looked at Jen and sighed.

'There is … a letter. Sybil left it with me when she knew she was dying. She made me make a promise that it shouldn't be handed over to Flora until Flora herself asks for it. You know our promises are binding.'

'Well, how can she ask for it if she doesn't know about it?' asked Jen, her chin jutting out in frustration.

'Sybil was very sure that she *would* know and we should trust that it would happen in its own good time. The right time.'

Jennet sat back, making an attempt to be satisfied with this as Sybil could not be disobeyed, even now. Yet as she sat back, Binky Peverel sat forward. As no words followed this, Peggy, who always addressed people by their given names as names endowed have a magic of their own, nodded to her.

'Bianca, what is it that you want to say?'

'Just that, well, if you were going to wait to tell her, you'd better hope that no one says anything before then. As I was leaving the inn…' she took a deep breath. 'Culhain came in.'

'Oh.'

Peggy stood up abruptly and headed for the door, worry etching even more lines on her face. Jen frowned.

' I know he's a fruit cake but he's only an old man. What harm can he do?'

'Have you ever managed to look at his face beneath that hood he always hides under?'

Peggy's intensity made Jen draw back as she shook her head. Peggy continued.

'Well, I have. Saw through the veil he summons up. He's been coming here every year since you were a child and in all that time he hasn't aged one bit.'

'You thought he might be a trickster at one time, Peggy. A Bodach' said Binky.

'He would have more disguises if he were. It's just that hood…' Peggy had her ideas of what he was hiding but she would probably never know.

Throwing a 'Blessed Be' over her shoulder to the others she made her way to the inn. She wondered how significant Culhain's visit on this day was. It couldn't be a coincidence. There was no such thing.

Chapter 6

<u>Culhain's Story</u>

Making her way to the Peverel Arms as fast as her arthritic legs would carry her, Peggy climbed up the two steps and into the old pub with its dark, low beams, imperfect with age. There was a fire in the old stone fireplace, unchanged for centuries.

All was as normal except, thought Peggy, for the tall figure standing at the bar with his back to her. As she watched, he slowly turned around to face her, As was usual, she only got an impression of his face. The same face she had seen and yet not seen, for years. The hood was still pulled up and around him and no one else in the bar seemed to think this was strange at all.

She shuddered but despite this, she stepped forward to have a word with him. Then she saw his head turn swiftly towards the closed outer door. Seconds later it opened and Flora walked through, an anxious expression on her face. Peggy closed her eyes. It was too late now. Things were already set in motion.

She walked to the furthest corner where she could keep an eye on Flora. She had promised Sybil that she would do just that. She was doing this for her friend's sake - and for the village.

She saw Flora go up to the bar and watched as her worried face slowly changed its expression and a smile passed over it. Mary might be a featherbrained chatterbox most of the time but she introduced normality and put you at your ease. She noted the similarity in looks between the two young women, apart from the hair colour and wondered if there was any truth in the persistent rumour of 'goings on' between Mary's great-grandmother and Flora's great-grandfather. This sort of thing went on and at one time was the norm in close-knit, isolated villages.

Mary nodded towards the table in the corner near the fire. Peggy made her way to the back of the room, making sure she could see both Flora and Culhain without Flora noticing her. In any case, Flora's attention was focused on the meal, which Mary had now put in front of her. As she ate the last mouthful, Peggy saw Flora's head turn towards the hooded man as he knocked loudly on the bar. He took a drink from the horn cup he carried with him and without further introduction, began to speak.

*

'The day was misty.' he began *'Light rain fell from the skies, much like today'.* Flora frowned and a man from the next table leaned over to her. 'The Storyteller' was all he said, as the hooded man continued to speak in his low mesmerising voice. *'This unnamed settlement was in its infancy and life was going about its daily grind. The farmer collected his crops with the help of the local people. The women brought their baking to the communal oven. The water was collected from the well and the wise woman collected her herbs for the healing of the people. The Elders gave advice and held ceremonies. Men and women met for their gathering once a week to discuss their business.*

The settlement held itself apart from other communities, with good reason - its very isolation made it unique. Yet in a time of scattered settlements, this place was special. Its connection to nature and the elements was strong, stronger than usual. Beyond the natural and into the supernatural. The reputation of supernatural entities in the place was such that outsiders kept away and it was left to its own devices.

On the rain-sodden moor surrounding the settlement, a stone portal had pushed through the peat. An entrance to another world – a Faerie world. Not a world of tiny creatures with gossamer wings and a magic wand – but another race of beings from a different plane of existence.

The Fairy Stone was what this village was named after. Farstone Village and Moor get their names from the Fae.

The Fae had the ability to appear right next to you and disappear just as quickly. When they let themselves be seen, the ordinary settlers were in awe of them. Their otherworldly looks, their superior knowledge and their ability to perform magic set them apart.

The Druids were the only ones brave enough to communicate with them and they spent hours in discussion with the Fae, gaining much of their knowledge from the Fairy Folk. This gave the Druids their reputation of wisdom and sorcery.

As time went by, although the Fae still had a presence in the village, they found themselves fading from the outer world. This was mainly because of stories of villagers' babies being snatched at birth and replaced with a Fae baby. The villagers said they could tell it was a changeling because the baby left in its place was ugly and nothing like their mother or father. As you can imagine, there were many reasons for them to use this excuse...

The storyteller sounded like he would have raised an eyebrow at this point if any eyebrows could be seen.

'Later, as the wise women took over from the Druids, who had almost disappeared. The Fae started to communicate with those women, who still believed in the Fae and happily existed alongside them. They all lived with the stories, true or not, of travellers disappearing and babies being snatched because, as both the Fae and the wicce knew, travellers and babies disappeared more by human hand than at the hands of the Fae.

Hilde the wise woman was the last great communicator before the Fae almost withdrew from this world – mostly just an unseen presence. Farstone was one of the last places left to them because of the belief of the people. They couldn't live in a world where times were moving so quickly that it didn't include them anymore - because the human brain refused to accept anything that it couldn't understand.

There was another pause

'But who am I to say there is no such thing as changelings or even halflings, which are half-Fae and half-human? Listen to my story and make up your own mind.

*

One day not so very long ago as Fae years go, a simple woman with no husband lived in the village. We shall call her Belle. When she was found to be with child, she swore a fairy lover had visited her as she slept on the moors. Most of the people in the village still accepted the Fae's existence although, knowing the woman, they doubted her story.

When the time for the birth arrived the midwife attended her. It was a difficult birth and both the mother and baby were almost lost. The baby was put to her breast to suckle but exhausted, the woman wanted nothing to do with it. So the midwife, who was also the foremost wise woman of the village, made up a life-preserving potion for the babe until he could be taken to a wet nurse.

The midwife left the room to let mother and baby sleep. She talked to Belle's mother who was worried about her daughter. Though never too bright, the pregnancy had made her state of mind worse. No, she had no idea who the father was either as the girl didn't mix with other people. As the mother had an inherited belief in the Fae's existence, she too was beginning to believe that the baby's father was from the Fae.

The next moment, a piercing scream came from Belle's room. Her face was white with terror. 'No no, take it away. They have stolen the baby and left the spawn of Cernunnos in his place. He has marked it. Take it away' she screamed

Cernunnos was known to be the King of the Fae around these parts. He was a god in Celtic culture but existed long before then, when the Earth was young, in times lost to us. Each class of Fae had its own King or Queen. Cernunnos was the horned King, a pair of antlers on top of his wild hair. He was most extraordinarily handsome. He was very tall, had jet black hair and eyes so black they pierced your soul. He had white skin and a robustness that put the old stories of gossamer-frail fairies to rest.

The midwife had to admit that the baby had all these physical attributes, apart from the horns – and it had already started to rally. Fearing what Belle would do to the child, she put him in a box, packed with blankets and took him into the warm kitchen where she too slept overnight.

Sometime later, the midwife awoke to find the baby had disappeared. She roused Belle's mother and after they realised that Belle had gone too, they went in search of the girl and her baby.

The mother knew that Belle often roamed the moors and they soon found her. She was on her way back to the farmhouse. She had been exposed to the cold and windy moors all night in her weakened state. All that she could say was she had left her baby on the moors for his father to look after.

Her mother half-dragged and half-carried Belle back to the house while the midwife went on searching for the baby. She knew there wasn't much chance of finding it alive but her compassion kept her searching.

Eventually, she came across an outcrop of rocks. The rocks formed a shelter and just inside that shelter, she found the baby. Incredibly he was alive and - the word came back to her from earlier – robust, as its cries on being picked up were enough to wake the Fae. Though they didn't. No Fae appeared.

The midwife worried that she shouldn't interfere in case it really was the son of Cernunnos. Worried that her beliefs would condemn a blameless human child to death, she made her decision. Her calling meant that she should preserve all living things if at all possible.

She returned with the baby to find that Belle had died ten minutes before. The child was brought up by Belle's mother and no further evidence apart from the physical resemblance ever linked him with the Fae.

However, it is said that Cernunnos regretted giving up his son, as he saw him grow into a healthy young man and not sickly like his mother. For the whole of the child's lifetime, he kept watch on his son at least once a year.

Even now on nights such as that of the boy's birth, with the mist rising from the ground, you will hear hoofbeats pass by you and see a fiery horse, flying furiously across the ground with the red-eyed, demon hound following.

Do not meet the eyes of the rider, the Fairy King. If you see him turn towards you - run – and keep running… or he could take you to the land of the Fae in place of his son. And you will be lost from this world forever.

*

As the storyteller finished his tale as abruptly as he started it, he turned to drink the dregs of his ale from the horn cup, which he then put back in one of his oversized pockets. His body turned towards Flora. She could see the glint of his eyes. She tried to see the rest of his face but at that moment the man made an ironic bow in her direction and then left the inn. Already shaken from both the encounter on the moors and the storybook equivalent she had just heard, she went up to the bar for liquid fortification.

'A bucket of white wine please' she said to Mary, who laughed. She probably was no younger than Flora herself- very early 20s perhaps- but she had the air of a mischievous child.

'Who was *that*?' Flora continued, giving an involuntary shiver.

'Colin' smiled Mary, who always seemed to be happy. 'Well really his name is something foreign-sounding but I can't pronounce it, so I call him Colin.'

'He's a little scary' Flora offered. 'He looks like a Jawa from Star Wars with his raggy clothes and big, hood and just a pair of eyes peering at you.'

'A what?'

'What?'

'You said he looks like a...something.'

' Oh, Jawa. You know? From Star Wars?' but from Mary's expression, she obviously didn't.

'He's a storyteller?'

'Yeah, comes here quite often and tells a few different stories. We think maybe he travels around the country, but nobody really knows. Brings that horn cup of his, fills it with ale twice, downs it, tells his story, then he's off. He doesn't pay for the ale, dad reckons he's earned it from his stories.'

'Does he often tell the black horse and rider tale? With a dog following it?'

' I think he's told it before? I don't actually listen to them now.'

'Only I've just seen him. The King of the Fairies. On his horse. With his dog. Looking for his son.' Flora shuddered. It just seemed too much of a coincidence, this story coming straight after she'd seen the rider. There must be an innocent explanation.

Flora's eyes were open wide but Mary's eyes were like saucers.

'You *didn't*! No wonder you looked scared when you came over. I would be too! Was he on a jet black steed, like Colin said?'

'It was a black horse, the rider had black hair, the dog was… No, the dog wasn't black but it was huge. sort of grey-coloured.'

' Oh, tell you who that could be then. The Folklore Man. Handsome as the Fairy King himself, rides the moors as fast as lightning. Still scary though.' Mary thought for a minute, 'Well he scares me anyway.'

'The Folklore Man?' Flora whispered to herself as Mary turned to serve another customer. These local legends were going to take some getting used to. Witches, Fairies, Storytellers, The Folklore Man, Demon Dogs... She might have to drink another large wine if she was going to sleep well tonight.

Peggy slipped out behind Flora, unnoticed by her. She overheard her telling Mary about her encounter on the moors. Interesting. She wasn't sure how she should feel about that. Pondering this, she stepped out and down onto the pavement. She was suddenly aware of a figure at her side.

'Blessed be' she addressed it.

'All is well?' asked Culhain.

' As can be.'

The figure paused in thought, then nodded.

' Things are as destiny intends' he said 'and the boy?'

'There too. Content. Enough so to be left to himself.'

'Still searching?'

'He'll always be searching -but in vain. For the best.'

Culhain sighed and then said,

'Yes, for the best'

Peggy nodded.

Culhain added, as an afterthought 'And the girl?'

Peggy smiled. 'You saw. It is good.'

'All will be well. The world is turning as it should be.'

And without her even noticing, he was gone.

Chapter 7

Waking refreshed after a surprisingly good night's sleep, all the ridiculous ideas of supernatural beings, fairies and witches had disappeared from Flora's mind. All she could think about now was getting into her cottage and getting her business sorted out.

Today was the day whatever possessions she had retained from her old home, were arriving in a small removal lorry. She wanted to see if the mattress from her old bed would fit on Sybil's bed. Luckily she found it did and she set about making the bed up with the brand new bedding she had bought in readiness.

She threw the windows open for most of the day to get some fresh air through. It didn't feel damp at all which was a good thing. At some point she would go into the nearest town and buy other bits and pieces she found she needed. Now she looked at her furniture in situ, she realised most of it could go in the store room or to the nearest charity shop as she liked the furniture that Sybil had left. It seemed to belong more in this cottage. Her furniture belonged to the three-bedroomed semi in suburbia it had come from. Maybe she could utilise some for her office and even in the shop.

By the end of the day, her mind was spinning. She had given the removal men, some sandwiches and a cuppa to see them home without a rumbly tummy but didn't feel like eating anything herself. She was too– was it excited or was it anxious?

A good brisk walk would do her good and the weather had stayed fine all day. She grabbed her raincoat again, just in case, but the breeze was gentle and the air was fresh as she made for the path she had taken yesterday up onto the moor.

This time when she reached the top of the first hill there was no horseman. Just a vast panorama of moorland as far as the eye could see. She had heard this moor was the largest in Yorkshire and she could well believe it. She saw ups and downs, hollows and hills, all spread out before her. She carried with her, as a townie, an idea of moorland being flat, so the occasional steeply rising hill before her was a revelation.

The moorland fell away over to the right and dipped down into a vale beyond, so she decided to make over that way. it would give her a good long walk and space to think about what she was going to do with the legacy Sybil had left her. She also needed to get to know her surroundings. After all, she would probably be on these moors more often than not. Hopefully, she would have time to stride across them, Bronte-like and not spend all her time chained to the business, as much as she was looking forward to starting it. The sale of her parent's house had given her enough to do the cottage up and to provide a small monthly amount to cushion her against any shortfall in earnings until the shop became established.

She wondered about opening the shop only for weekends and perhaps Thursdays and Fridays and devoting the rest to looking after the wildflower meadow and her online business. She had wanted to call it Natural Healing, which did what it said on the tin – but she was toying with bringing the wildflower aspect into it in some way. These and many other ideas occupied her thoughts as she walked on.

Her mind was feeling particularly fertile at the moment as she not only worked out what decorating/repairing needed to be done at the cottage but also how she could persuade the locals to use her for minor aches and pains, colds and coughs, love potions– The last thought came unbidden to her and made her laugh until she realised how dark it had become in what she thought was a short space of time.

She was only vaguely aware that it was raining but as she came to a halt, she saw the rain start to beat down more heavily. She pulled her hood up and lifted her eyes to see the reason for the sudden darkness. Storm clouds hovered above her, low and threatening. She had been so deep in thought planning her future in Farstone that she hadn't noticed a thing.

She took out her phone to check the time and realised it was almost two hours since she had left her cottage - and she had been walking in one direction, away from it. She turned slowly in a circle to get her bearings and realised with an unpleasant thump of the heart that there was nothing but moorland all around her with no landmark that she could recognise. She didn't realise she had gone this far. She didn't know the moor at all and didn't even know the direction she was going.

There was no network on her phone for the sat nav. She found the compass was working but as she stared at the pointer it started spinning like crazy so she couldn't rely on that either. Did she even know which compass direction the village was? She tried to think of which windows the sun shone in at what time of day, but her brain wouldn't work.

She took a deep breath to calm her thoughts. Perhaps if she just retraced her steps in the direction she had come, she would eventually reach home. To her horror, she had no idea which direction that was. She had turned in circles trying to find signs of habitation or a landmark and was completely disorientated. Now everywhere looked the same. The rain was falling heavily now, battering down on her hood, sounding like a drumbeat in her ears. Staring down at the bracken-covered ground, she tried to identify the sheep track she had used. There were too many of them. Some of them crisscrossing the others. She straightened up and shook her head at her foolishness.

There was one thing - standing here like the proverbial lost sheep wasn't going to help her.

Checking her phone again for reception and finding none, she set off in what she hoped was the right direction relying on instinct alone. The clouds were threatening now, heralding a storm. Night was falling anyway, but the low oppressive sky had brought darkness too early.

She was used to and enjoyed Star Walking. The feeling of freedom it gave her being out at night and feeling the cold air on her cheeks. Of being out when others weren't. Yet that was in places she was familiar with and by the light of the stars or the moon. Tonight, no moon or stars were visible and - listening to the first distant rumble of thunder - the only light she could expect to show her the way tonight would be flashes of lightning.

Cursing her stupidity, she set off in her chosen direction with her head down so she didn't trip and occasionally lifted her head to look for signs of habitation. Any lights from a friendly house – in the middle of a forbidding and unfriendly moor... She realised this wasn't going to be likely as she hadn't passed any.

The driving rain forced her head down again. Half an hour later, there was still nothing. Nothing but darkness and desperation now. She could almost be in the bowels of Hell except at least there the flames would be lighting her way and keeping her warm. Her imagination started overtaking her common sense and she could almost see little red imps with forked tails dancing around, laughing at her–

This was no good, she thought, bringing herself up sharp. Carefully planting her feet, she turned her body around in each direction for a sign of civilisation. Nothing. The wind had increased along with the storm and was now howling around her body, making it hard to keep upright.

The thunder had gradually crept nearer until it was almost overhead. Thunder didn't bother her. She quite enjoyed hearing the majesty of nature. Usually at least. What was bothering her was this awful, incessant rainstorm of biblical proportions. There wasn't one inch of her that wasn't soaking wet through. There hadn't even been anything for her to shelter under or against. There was just a vast expanse of rolling moorland as far as she could see, which wasn't actually very far at the moment.

Then the lightning flashed. She stopped moving and watched mesmerised as it lit up the sky and then zig-zagged down towards the ground to whatever had drawn it down. Flora heard herself whimpering as if from a long way away. Thunder didn't bother her but lightning did. Lightning on a wide open moor, looking for something to earth it. She thought of her coat zip, her rings, the gold chain around her neck, and the coins she kept in her pocket just in case.

And then she began to panic, spinning round in a grotesque parody of a folk dance - her arms spread out and her face towards the sky so that the rain forced her eyes shut with its ferocity. She asked whoever was listening, perhaps the perverse weather gods with a strange sense of humour, to help her. Then she gave a strangled laugh and sat down on one of the many sheep tracks, rain flowing along it like a river. She put her head on her knees and cried tears of self-pity. She knew that she alone was to blame.

A crack of thunder echoed around the heathland and simultaneously a spectacular display of light illuminated the night sky. Flora curled up into a tight ball and just looked up in time to see the lightning fork strike the ground on top of a hill to her left. Incredibly, she saw silhouetted there, some sort of a ruin. A barn perhaps, that had fallen into disuse as not even the sheep wanted to come out to this Godforsaken place. She didn't care. It was her first chance of some sort of shelter, so in the sure and certain conviction that lightning doesn't strike twice in the same place, she made her stumbling way across to where she'd seen the glowing ruin.

Chapter 8

Holding the exact position in her sight, Flora made for the shelter. In truth, it was mostly intuition as the night was so black that she almost wished for another flash of lightning to light her way. On second thoughts, she didn't want to provide a metal-carrying, moving target for the lightning so, staring fixedly at the point where she hoped she had seen the structure, she tripped and stumbled her way forward.

She was upon it before she realised and got her foot caught in some sort of creeping plant, sending her sprawling across the ground. She raised her head to see, not six inches in front of her, a solid block of stone. Thanking whoever had started looking after her tonight, she pulled herself up and looked around. Shapes and shadows were all she could see. She chanced using her phone torch. There was still no reception and she wondered if a mast had been struck. For good measure she aimed the beam up into the sky, waving it about for a while. Although it was the logical thing to do at this stage, she was strangely reluctant to bring the moors rescue service out in this weather and put them in danger for some idiot woman who should have read the weather signs much better- and kept a weather-eye out as she was walking. She had been so intent on her plans that she had noticed nothing around her.

Bringing the torch beam down to earth, she focused on the ruins and was surprised to see it wasn't a dilapidated shippen but a standing stone, right here in the middle of the moors. Not just one stone but three. Two uprights and a large capstone across the top. She'd seen them before at Stonehenge. Were they called megaliths? No,– dolmens. It seemed strange that the structure was here in the middle of nowhere but she was glad it was. She would shelter underneath from the rain and hopefully, the capstone would deflect any more lightning strikes away from her.

She stepped down onto a smooth pathway heading to the space between the stones. It looked well-worn. Perhaps sheep took their shelter here as well. She was suddenly aware of a looming shape to her left, bending over and standing and then bending again in the howling gale. She flinched, as though under attack, then gave a maniacal laugh when she realised it was an old thorn tree, bending against the prevailing wind. Hawthorn or Blackthorn probably, as they could withstand any conditions.

Training the torch again on the stones, she headed for their shelter. In the torchlight she saw the creeper had made its way up and over the stones, giving them an otherworldly appearance. What seemed to be honeysuckle wound its way up one side, the tendrils reaching up towards the swirling black sky. On the other side, she could see hips from the sweet briar rose curling around the right-hand stone and up over the capstone. She wondered vaguely why the hips were out at this time of year. It was completely incongruous on a wild barren part of the vast moor.

She entered the ancient shelter. Strangely, it went much further back than she first thought. Almost like the start of a tunnel. She hesitated. She didn't want to go any further for some reason. It might be sensible to get further inside the shelter, but something told her not to. Perhaps the stone wasn't as stable there and might collapse? She always listened to her instincts and if she didn't want to step further into the shelter, then she would make do just inside the stones. Anything would be better than this constant, unrelenting deluge.

She settled against the stone on her right. The honeysuckle cushioning her back and the tendrils reaching down over her shoulder. She smiled wryly. Trusting her instincts? What happened to her instincts when she set off earlier for her 'short walk' on the moors? She always believed that everything happened for a reason, but for the life of her, she couldn't imagine a reason for her predicament tonight.

Sitting there curling herself up against the cold, another half hour passed, at the end of which she had started to shiver and was now shaking violently. She was soaked to the skin and whereas the shelter gave her some relief against the rain, it wasn't drying her. The night would get colder and her lack of movement would contribute to the intense cold she was beginning to feel. If only she knew in which direction she should walk.

She took out her phone for the compass again but it was even worse than before, spinning round wildly – perhaps the stone was affecting it? The rumble of the thunder was still there but some distance away and the lightning was further away too. Thinking of Culhain's story, she worried that she had more chance of dying of hypothermia tonight than of getting struck by lightning. So with more hope than expectation, she edged out again into the rainstorm and tried to see through the water cascading into her eyes.

She blinked and wiped her hand across her eyes and then blinked again. There in the distance - was it a light? Very small and very weak but it *was* a light even though Flora turned away and then back in case it was an illusion that would disappear. She wiped her eyes again. It was still there. A watery, weak glow but it was the most welcome sight Flora had ever seen. Forcing her now aching limbs to work again, she propelled herself towards the beacon of hope.

Chapter 9

Half running, half stumbling through the open gateway, Flora made for the main door of the farmhouse. There were barns to her left and the stable over to her right where she could hear ominous banging and crashing noises. Even though she could see a dim light burning there, she kept well away and made for the comfort of the light in the window to the left of the main door.

She knocked very loudly as the wind was making so much noise whipping around these walls, that it would be hard to make herself heard. She tried again and then knocked on the window. This time there was a scuffling thumping noise behind the door, then silence.

Suddenly the thunder echoed in her ears. At the same time, there was a loud bang at the other side of the door and the noises in the stable became deafening. The snorts and bellowing of an angry or frightened horse, kicking against its confines. What if it got out?

She renewed her knocking with the rain trying to outdo her with its assault on the door. Oh, hang this, she thought and, grabbing the handle, put her shoulder against the door. It was already unlocked and as it ricocheted back from the inside wall, Flora found herself flattened against it by an enormous creature that then sped out of the house and across the yard.

She screamed. The piercing scream of abject terror. She started to make for the stable in preference to finding any more huge creatures in the house. Was this a house of demons, worthy of the Storyteller's tales? She was halfway across when she saw the light in the stable move and come out into the yard. Her eyes fixed themselves on the large storm lantern, hovering in midair before its position changed and revealed the person holding it.

She almost screamed again, but it stuck in her throat. The man appeared to be a giant. His floor-length black coat flapped around his long legs and his black hair blew into his eyes and stayed there, plastered to his forehead with rain. He lifted the lantern higher, taking a couple of steps towards her. Under his thick black brows, she saw his black eyes flash in the light, looking as angry and as violent as the horse had sounded. She had landed in Hell. She tried to step back but found she couldn't move. She was rooted to the ground. He came to within a few steps of her and held the light forward to see her face.

'Who the *hell* are you?' he spat.

The air crackled between them for what seemed like minutes before she could manage to reply.

'I only wanted shelter.'

She could hear herself whining and hated herself for it.

' I just wanted to come into your house for a while.'

'Don't you *dare* cross that threshold!' he shouted at her and then suddenly noticed the open door. He shouted a name out that must be the creature, she thought.

'Why have you let my dog out?' he shouted at her. 'Which way did he go?'

'Dog? That was a dog?' Flora frowned, then pointed in the direction of the barn to the left.

The 'demon' in front of her started running with long-legged strides towards the barn, while Flora looked towards the open door. She would rather face whatever was making that noise in the stable than go through that door to face any other creatures that may be waiting to jump out at her. She walked across to her right.

As she entered she found a large, ebony black horse, streaked with foam. His eyes were wild and going back into his head. He reared up, then pawed the ground with his hooves, shrieking horribly. There was a smaller lantern on the floor in front of her. She could see by that light that the horse had all but destroyed the wood at the front of its stable. Poor thing, it was terrified.

Flora used to go riding when she was young and remembered one highly-strung horse who hated anyone coming near him to saddle him up. He was uncontrollable. He only calmed down when the owner of the riding stables let Flora go in and talk to him. She got a reputation as a sort of teenage amateur horse-whisperer. Stallions were always more uncontrollable and she suspected this one was a stallion too. Perhaps if she just…

'Come on now boy, the noise will be gone soon. It won't hurt you, I promise. Can I come and talk to you?'

Her voice was low and soft and she held her hand towards him palm up. The horse's eyes stopped swivelling and tried to focus on this new sound. He pawed the ground now but didn't rear.

'That's right boy. That's so good. Nobody wants to harm you. We're on your side.'

He looked at her sidewards, still mistrustful but the pawing decreased. Now she was with him, she wasn't afraid at all. Her hand went slowly but surely to his neck where she made short, stroking movements, rhythmical and constant.

'There, I told you so.'

The thunder rumbled again and he pulled back but she kept the pressure there on his neck and carried on talking to him calmly.

'The storm is further away now. I don't think it will come back. It's only a sound in the sky now, going away from you. Nothing will hurt you. I promise.'

Her other hand reached out to gently stroke the horse's great head. He snorted and pulled back but she continued talking and stroking until at last he gave a resigned snicker and pushed his nose into her hand in a conciliatory gesture. She smiled.

'There, you softie. Let's get you wiped down now.'

With unhurried movements so as not to frighten him, she opened the battered stable door, lifted the blanket from over it and began to methodically wipe the sweat and foam from his coat. She had been aware of another presence for a while but was too involved in calming the horse. Her attention had to be focused solely on what she was doing. Any lack of concentration and she would have lost him.

Now, however, as she knew the horse was alright, the focus had worn off and she felt a prickle at the back of her head. Trying not to show tension in front of the horse, she finished what she was doing, exited the stable door and hung the blanket back over it. Only then did she turn to see the black-clad man in the doorway. The angry demonic expression replaced by a look of complete and absolute amazement.

Chapter 10

The man had led her into his house after that. Flora could now see, walking behind him, that he wasn't some evil giant but a tall man around six feet three if she were to guess. He had yet to say a word. He had just beckoned. She said goodbye to the horse who nuzzled her shoulder. The man blinked and looked puzzled, then he turned towards the farmhouse where she found herself now.

    They walked to the end of the long passage, passing a door on the left with an oil lamp in the window, placed on a desk in what looked like an office. The light she had seen when she was on the moor perhaps, although it didn't seem to give off much light. She felt she had gone back in time with all these oil lamps. He carried on to a door on the right which opened out onto a warmly lit kitchen. She was surprised to see that the kitchen was completely modern. There were brand new units, modern copper light fittings and the latest range oven. There was also an ancient black-leaded range, used, it seemed, mostly for the fire that was now burning brightly in the open grate. The modernity seemed somehow out of place with its situation high on the moors.

She saw the light was coming from oil lanterns. He lit two large candles placed on the table and seeing her watching this action with a puzzled expression, he explained.

'Power cut – generator problems' he said. Short and sweet but it was an explanation. Then he grunted again.

'You're dripping all over the floor.'

She didn't stop to question how this was phrased but took it as a criticism.

'That's probably because I've been wandering the moor throughout the storm. Lost, scared, freezing-cold, and strangely enough, dripping wet - and I became colder and wetter since the owner of the farmhouse forbade me to go inside it.'

Her voice had risen in indignation towards the end of this little speech and she stuck her chin out towards him in defiance. He seems to be taking a deep breath possibly to calm himself. It didn't work.

'Just think about it for a minute, will you?' he said in a dangerously low voice, 'It's nighttime. There's the worst storm I've known in years raging out there. No sane person would be out in it. This farm is in the middle of nowhere and suddenly... you're confronted with a spectral grey figure, with long black hair plastered to her head, luminous pale eyes shining in the light of the lantern and a dreadful expression on her face. Did you expect me to invite you in for tea and scones?'

His voice had risen too now and his eyes stared into hers with an indignant expression. Almost black eyes, Flora thought as she stared back into them but with hints of brown in the lamplight. His mouth and jaw were set and his chiselled cheekbones twitched in anger. Something floated into her mind. Spoken in Mary's voice. Good looking Folklore Man.

'You're the Folklore Man – and you are just a man, not a spirit of the moor.'

He laughed scornfully.

'Hang on before you start laughing at me. You said, "Don't you dare cross that threshold!" Did you think *I* was a spirit?'

Her mouth twitched as she said this. He gave a resigned sigh.

'I thought you were the Grey Lady who is supposed to wander the moors. I saw you yesterday didn't I?'

She nodded.

'Or you could have been a witch.'

He gave a rather disarming apologetic smile now.

'That's okay. I thought you were a demon from Hell with a devil dog and a spectral horse.'

They looked at each other and started to laugh. He shook his head.

'Come on, let's get you out of those wet clothes.'

She teased him again with a look of mock horror on her face. He looked embarrassed, totally at odds with his strong and masterful attitude earlier.

'I would love to. Have you got anything I can change into, please?'

He disappeared into a room across the hallway, reappearing a couple of minutes later. He walked to a large kettle on the range hot plate.

'I've put some of my things on the bed and I'll put this hot water into the sink in the bathroom. No bath tonight I'm afraid, but at least it will warm you up a little.'

He walked back, with the kettle, into the bedroom and through it into what must be the bathroom en suite. He obviously didn't have - or want - many visitors. Ten minutes later, warmed up slightly and with her hair towelled as dry as she could, she went back through to the kitchen with her wrung-out clothes. She had washed her underwear and would try and put it in an inconspicuous place to dry. The other things, including her coat, were put over a drying rack and winched towards the ceiling in front of the range.

The man handed over a very welcome cup of tea and introduced himself as Calum Hythe.

'Normally known as Cal. I am indeed the folklore man and blessed with an overactive imagination. I don't know whether I was more terrified of you being a witch or a grey lady - or more excited that I had met one of them.'

He smiled ruefully.

' I'm Flora Goode - and you do know witches don't look like the old pictures in storybooks, don't you?'

'What? With a long dark cloak and long black hair?' An ironic smile appeared on his face as he looked at her hair, spread across her shoulders.

'The 'cloak' was a showerproof coat from my local outdoor camping and hikers shop. I now know why it says showerproof and not torrential-storm-proof. So- every woman with long black hair is a witch?'

'Of course not. I gather stories and legends. I get carried away sometimes. I promise you, I'm not a modern-day witch hunter.'

He looked up at her. He'd obviously heard the stories circulating in the village, famous for its witches. That was just history though, wasn't it?

'You're just wanting to know the old stories then?'

'Not just the old stories.' He frowned. 'Are you from the village?'

'I've just moved here. My great aunt - well I call her a great aunt - left me her cottage and shop in her will.'

'The Gallipot place?' He leaned towards her, suddenly interested.

'Yes, her name was Sybil Gardwicke.'

'The Wildflower Witch?'

'Maybe…? But she wasn't a witch, she was a healer. That's what all the flowers were for. If she made potions they were just using the ingredients that are present in a lot of modern-day medicines, to help to heal people. She didn't have a broomstick or a cat as far as I know. Unless it was just for sweeping the yard. With the broomstick, not the cat.' she finished.

'I'm well aware of it' he smiled disarmingly, 'I'm wanting to write a history of The Witches of Farstone but a cloak of silence has been spread over the locals and I'm being blocked at every turn. I don't think they like me very much.'

He shrugged his shoulders. Flora didn't think it would bother him if he was liked or not unless it stopped him from getting his own way.

'Maybe if you let the people know it would be a sympathetic history, not a sensationalist history.?'

'I don't write sensationalist nonsense, it's always impeccably researched and sympathetic. It's not just a history though.'

'You mean there are still witches there?'

'Of course, there are witches everywhere. But this village has a tradition of witchcraft which is the strongest and longest-lasting in England, and the superstition is that they are not allowed to die out or the village will fail. I don't believe your great-aunt was the last one. Have you come to take her place? Are you a witch?'

He said it jokingly but his eyes were serious.

'Of course not, or I've never thought of myself that way at least. I'm a healer – and although I've now been told she was a healer too, I only actually met her once.'

Calum seemed to consider for a moment.

'You're no relation to the bookshop woman then? You look a little like her.'

' No relation at all thank goodness' she said, thinking of her reception.

A noise from a low open door at the back of the room made her jump. It was a sort of a strangled howl.

'What the…!'

'My dog Finn, the one you nearly loosed onto the moors.'

'Was that really a dog?'

' Yes, that was a dog. Although anyone would be forgiven for thinking he was a large blob of jelly.'

'Oh, most dogs are scared of storms' she said sympathetically.

'This one is scared of his own shadow' he laughed.

Flora looked over to the black space inside what looked like a broom cupboard. She could just make out two eyes shining in the candlelight.

'You'll have to stay here tonight. The rain is still coming down in torrents and the track will be a river. Besides which, I couldn't leave Finn on his own or take him with me for that matter. You can have my room. I'll sleep on this chair.'

Flora thanked him with no hesitation. She felt strangely safe with him now, compared to her initial feelings on first seeing him. She stood up and turned towards the whimpering noises.

'Come on' she said in the direction of the cupboard.

'It's no good. He won't leave the safety of his den for anyone tonight. You may have calmed my horse, which I still can't believe by the way, but you will have a harder job getting Finn to come near you. He's very nervous around other people, especially when there's been a thunderstorm.'

'Finn, come on. It's all right. Come and get warm.'

' He won't–' Calum stopped as the huge grey and damp Irish wolfhound unfolded himself from the cupboard and made tentative steps with his big clumpy paws in Flora's direction. He stopped just in front of her so she gently sat down on the chair and held her hand out, talking to him softly all the time. He came forward. Calum sat there open-mouthed, hardly daring to breathe.

'You *are* a witch' he whispered.

She looked up at him and he noticed her attractive pale grey eyes and the way her mouth dimpled when she smiled at him.

' I have a way with animals, always have had. I'm calm around them and can empathise with them.'

She kept talking to Finn who put his nose against Flora's hand and nudged it before sitting down in front of her.

Calum shook his head in amazement as Finn put his great head on her lap in a touching show of trust.

*

The next morning all signs of the storm had vanished and an azure blue sky looked down upon a rain-washed moorland. Calum had said he would take Flora down to the village in his four-track, which was hidden inside the larger barn but the mud track was still awash with flowing rivulets. He took her over the crest of one of the hills immediately behind his farmhouse and from there he pointed straight down to where she could see the roofs of village houses in the distance.

'If you follow the sheep tracks directly, it leads you back to the wood behind your Cottage. I use it sometimes if I'm walking. It cuts a mile off the distance so that it's only two miles as the crow flies. It leads around the edge of the wood, past Peggy Harker's place and down to the track opposite the inn. *You* can just wander down through Pookey wood though, seeing as you own it.'

Flora thanked him profusely. After a very shaky start, they found they had a lot of common interests and had talked well into the night. At the moment, wearing her own dry but muddy clothes, she couldn't wait to get home and have a bath.

She had gone earlier into the stable to say goodbye to Fury who was thankfully calm after his ordeal and was waiting to be fed. Now, she said goodbye to Finn who looked sad to see his new friend go. She cast a look over her shoulder then turned fully around with her back to the farmhouse, shielding her eyes from the sun. Calum looked puzzled.

'What are you looking for?'

'Oh, nothing. I just took shelter by some rocks but I can't see them now. I think they might be just beyond that ridge' she frowned. 'Anyway, please call into Gallipot cottage if you're in the village, won't you?'

' I will. I don't come in often as I'm writing a book at the moment - but yes, I will see you again.'

I hope so at least, he thought as he watched her stride out towards the village.

He's definitely not a demon, thought Flora, as she turned back and waved.

Chapter 11

The joy of living alone was that you didn't have anyone to worry about you and you didn't have to worry about anyone else. There were downsides to this. She had called the inn as soon as she got phone reception on her way back down, to apologise for not letting them know about the room, in case they had been worried about her. They hadn't even realised she wasn't there. So much for help coming out to her on the moors.

No one had realised she'd spent the night out there. She could have been found three days later wandering the moors lost and completely out of her wits. Or even dead, like Belle in the story. As she had been saved from all this by a tall, dark, handsome and devilish stranger though, she could just slip down to her back kitchen door, slide in and put the kettle on as normal.

'Where do you think you've been?'

The aggrieved voice of Peggy greeted her as she made her way through the wildflowers which brushed their damp heads against her hands. Peggy had been peering through the kitchen window and now stood legs akimbo and hands planted on ample hips.

Flora was torn between being glad someone had missed her after all and being annoyed that they were angry with her after her ordeal.

'I've been lost on the moor in the middle of last night's storm' she said sharply. 'I was cold, wet, miserable and could have died.'

Peggy didn't change her expression.

'What sort of idiot goes out on the moor when a storm is threatening?' she asked with what seemed like genuine curiosity.

'An idiot who has lived in a town all her life and isn't used to country ways. When we're out walking and there's a storm we pop into the nearest cafe or catch a bus home. *That* kind of idiot.'

'You acknowledge you *were* an idiot then? When you said you could have died, it was very close to the truth. There's not much shelter out there.'

Peggy nodded at the door during this speech expecting Flora to open it. On their short acquaintance, she had come to realise that Peggy either kept ominously quiet or told the whole blunt and unvarnished truth.

Flora unlocked the door then rooted in a box that was on the table, coming out with a kettle, two cups, tea bags and powdered milk, the last of which Peggy turned her nose up at. This was the emergency box with essentials she had brought in the car.

After a few minutes of silence while she made the tea – Peggy didn't speak as she seemed to be waiting for an answer to her question - Flora pushed the steaming black tea across to her.

'I was too preoccupied with what I was going to do with the cottage, the business, my life... I do have a lot on my mind you know? I hadn't looked at the weather forecast. What's more, because I was deep in thought, I hadn't read the signs. I hadn't felt the wind change or the feeling in the air. I hadn't seen the sky turning slowly to a forbidding...

'And you can usually read the signs?' Peggy seemed more animated.

'I – well, yes. I think so. I like the weather changes. I take an interest in it. Maybe it's because it's Yorkshire and further up north that it took me by surprise this time. Anyway, yes Peggy, I was an idiot and I won't be doing it again in a hurry, not without reading the signs anyway.'

Peggy let a smile flit across her face. Flora looked her in the eye.

'Did you miss me then? I didn't know you cared.'

She gave the older woman a sweetly innocent smile. Peggy tutted.

'I called at the inn but you weren't there. Mary thought you might be at home but your car is still in the car park. I had to trust to Nature that you would be safe. I certainly wasn't going to roam on the moors looking for you' she paused. 'So did you find shelter then?'

'I did eventually. At the farmhouse with Culhain's fairy demon rider and his terrible, ferocious hound. After thinking at first that I would rather face a slow death on the moors, than the temper of the rider and his horse, I found them all agreeable. In the end, I managed to calm down both the horse and the dog.'

'You did?'

'Yes. Sybil said that I had the gift when she left my parent's house when I was seven. It's the thing I remember most about her visit. Next door's uncontrollable dog snapped, snarled and barked at everyone as usual, when we went out into the front garden to see her off. Yet it loved me and wagged its tail when I went over to stroke it. Sybil was very impressed. She asked if I was like that with people too.'

'Mmm. And are you?'

'Not as much but I'd like to think I can empathise with people when they need me to. Anyway, he let me sleep in his bed for the night.'

Peggy had a straight face but there was a slight shift of her right eyebrow.

'He wasn't in it at the time' Flora laughed, 'he was in the kitchen sleeping on the comfy chair. '

'The folklore man who wants to write about the Witches of Farstone?' Peggy asked in a slightly dismissive tone.

'Yes, He's a little eccentric perhaps.' Flora answered, aware that possibly most of the village folk she had met so far could be described as such.

'You don't believe in witches then?'

Peggy grunted as she eased her aching knees into a standing position and waited for her answer.

'The modern-day concept? Yes. There are women today who do a similar thing to what I intend to do. They heal, they read the signs in situations, they believe there is more to this world than we can see - and they work with Nature. So if they are witches, yes, I believe in them. If you want to give them' she stopped '–us, I suppose, a label. I imagine Sybil was a healer but in that case, she could be called a witch too. Cal said she was called the Wildflower Witch around here.'

Peggy allowed a smile to reach her eyes.

'She was. Cal?' she asked, 'On familiar terms then?'

'Well, after you've slept in his bed you feel almost obliged to find out his first name' she winked.

The wheeze of a laugh came from Peggy. Flora was beginning to recognise her little idiosyncrasies.

'Come around when you're ready, if you have any questions about Sybil. And it wasn't really your fault, the storm was sudden and wasn't forecast, which is curious… Anyway, I'm very glad you didn't expire on the moors' she smiled.

Flora grinned back.

'I might have done if I hadn't come across the stones on the hill above the farmhouse first.'

' Stones?' Peggy stopped abruptly and turned, overbalancing slightly as Flora put a hand out to steady her.

'Yes, they gave a bit of shelter because they had a large stone balanced across the top of two others. I tried to get dry but I was already too wet. Then I saw the farmhouse when the lightning flashed again, thank goodness.'

Peggy frowned.

'Stones in the middle of the moor?'

'Yes, I know it sounds weird and I couldn't see exactly where they were when I left this morning. They were like, you know, that stone structure at Stonehenge that looks like a huge door. This was much smaller but…'

Flora stopped talking and watched, puzzled as Peggy moved down the grass driveway without another word.

*

Peggy burst into the bookshop and went up to the startled figure behind the counter.

'Jennet, get hold of Bianca. We have to call a gathering at the Folly. Flora found the Fae portal and we have to discuss what this means'

Chapter 12

Flora spent the next few weeks getting her cottage, her garden and her life sorted. None of them needed as much doing as she first thought. She had prepared herself for months of work but the cottage was in better condition than she had first thought. The garden was way beyond her expectations.

Consequently, her life was so much easier. Peggy had told her that the roof had been mended two years before Sybil died and she had kept up with most of the repairs too. Apart from the obvious ones that Flora had noticed when she arrived. Flora wondered if it was because she knew she was passing it on to her. It seemed like that might be the case.

Nevertheless, after the gutter was repaired, the paintwork, the paint and the plaster work needed freshening up - so she had the decorators in to paint all the walls white and brighten it up. It was all a faded cream which may or may not have been white to start with. The walls above the fires were black with soot and she felt it was rather a shame to get rid of the history. Still, she would be using the fires again and would make her own impression on the fireplace walls in good time.

While the decorators were in, she kept out of the way by exploring her new and exciting garden. She wandered up and down the main path and across the many little narrow paths between them. She collected seeds to use again and snipped off flower heads of lavender to dry. She pulled out any weeds but was surprised at how remarkably weed-free it was. What were weeds anyway? A flower in the wrong place, as the saying goes.

More often than not. She carried a book with her. One of the many books she had found on the single shelf above Sybil's desk. With her herbal training, Flora could recognise most of the flowers and herbs that populated the meadow, but there were quite a few she had never seen before.

To her delight, she found that Sybil had kept a detailed watercolour sketch of every flower she had found in her meadow, alongside a description of its qualities, What it was used for, how it was applied or administered and, very important to Flora, how effective she had found the remedy. Many of Sybil's book entries were already known and used by Flora but Sybil knew so many more ways of healing with the plants and flowers. The old ways, ones that had been used for hundreds of years. She had even mentioned the Hilde from Culhain's story.

She had lived in the eleventh century and her potions and methods had been copied into this book to be handed down through the years. There was an underlined note next to the mention of Hilde saying *'These remedies still work!'*.

Again Flora wondered if these notes were written for her benefit as it seemed she was the one entrusted now to carry these recipes on. She suddenly felt very humble when she realised this and was so glad that she was in the position to put it all into practice.

This brought her up short. It was too much of a coincidence that she had chosen the same path as a woman she had only met once. Had anything been said at that one meeting to set her on this course? She racked her brains but couldn't recall anything. She had only been left alone with her briefly in the back garden while her mother had gone to make tea. She could remember showing her some flowers and talking about them and Flora had picked some daisies for Sybil. Then she had made herself a daisy chain. That's all. Surely that couldn't have been it?

In another book from the shelf. She found information on how to take care of a wildflower meadow, again with copious underlined notes next to paragraphs. Sometimes *'Yes, that works'* or occasionally *'No! At least not in these conditions.'*

Flora could see both these books becoming her horticultural bibles. There was another large book, not on the small shelf but on one of the bigger bookshelves against the wall. It was leather-covered and was as tall and as thick as an encyclopaedia. Inside it were hundreds of written recipes. Potions and salves, remedies for all occasions. They were written in different inks and handwriting, the work of more than one person.

Flora had looked at some of the earlier entries, handling the book reverently, and had found a couple of them were potentially dangerous. She would look them up before she wrote them off but realised that we knew and understood things today that these people didn't, all that time ago. There were long-term effects that, even if they were healed of one thing at that time, could potentially have given them something worse.

She was extremely careful, by instinct and training and she would weed these out. There didn't appear to be many, thankfully, that she herself wouldn't use today. She had her own extensive notes for the book she was hoping to write when she had time but these books were a wonderful discovery. This whole cottage and its garden was a treasure trove for someone like herself.

Boxes had been delivered and stored in the newly decorated shop. They contained paper packets which she would use to send culinary herbs or calming herbs through the post along with her own recipe herbal teas. She had made a couple of trips to the nearest market town of Beck Isle to get new throws, cushions and more bedding. She had bought some new cushion covers but Sybil's crocheted and embroidered ones were beautiful, so she washed them carefully and would reuse them.

When the paint dried she finished unpacking her bits and bobs and eventually, the place began to look like home. The little black and white kitten she had seen on the first day had also made her home here. She had named it Freya, which was approved with a purr. Flora wondered if it belonged to any of her neighbours, but extensive enquiries had proved this wasn't the case. She was told that there were usually odd cats running around here and there, products of feline liaisons up at the farm that operated independently now, alongside Peverel Hall.

The kitten wasn't the only visitor. Peggy popped in a few times, making friends with the cat. Peggy remarked on the name, telling her that she knew her Norse mythology. They had more in common than Flora had realised and she came to enjoy her visits.

Mary popped down every couple of days bringing a sandwich from her mum and with a message to go to the Peverel arms for a free meal while her house was being invaded by workmen.

The lady who she had seen in the inn on the first night had been in the bar again the next time Flora went in. A frequent visitor perhaps? She had hugged Flora and squeezed her shoulders as though she knew her well. A week later, she had come round shouting over the hedge at the bottom of her driveway when Flora was in the garden. She was Lady Bianca Peverel and had invited her up to the Hall for a coffee. As there were workmen spilling out of both the shop and the kitchen doorways at the time, Flora promised her she would be there as soon as all this was finished.

Even Cal had popped around briefly, ostensibly to find out how she was settling in. He also asked her if she could come up to his farmhouse sometime to show him where the rocks she had sheltered under in the storm had been. She promised him too, that she would do that when things had eased off here. Meanwhile, she invited him into the garden to show him exactly why Sybil had been called the Wildflower Witch. He was very impressed and looked around the meadow in wonder. She watched him and thought how different he was now from the fierce monster she had first met. In attitude at least. The dark, brooding good looks were still there. Unfortunately.

The only unfriendly person in the whole village was the woman from the bookshop who made a point of leaving when Flora went in. Her husband was still nice though and helped to find whatever book she had been searching for.

Now, everything was done. As she sat at Sybil's desk first thing in the morning to write a list of supplies out, she felt very happy in her lovely new home. She felt as though she belonged and always had done. Her biro had out of ink and there were only broken pencils on the desk. She would have put 'more biros' down on her list if she had anything to write with.

She tried again to get the narrow drawer just above the leather desk surface, to open. It had been stuck ever since she arrived. She jiggled it about a bit. She didn't want to prise it with a knife or a screwdriver as the desk was an antique and too lovely to damage. There wasn't even a keyhole so it couldn't be locked. Was it a secret drawer? She laughed to herself. That only usually happened in murder mysteries, the place where a gun was found. Despite that, she pressed all the knobbly bits at the side and above the drawer.

Suddenly one of the carvings gave way under her fingers and the drawer shot out. Well I never, she thought with a grin. Still no pens though, although there was something. She peered in and took out a small thick envelope. It had her name on it. *Flora* - in the same handwriting Sybil had used in the books. Frowning, she slit the letter open and saw many pages packed with neat handwriting. She read the first lines and then put the letter back in the envelope with trembling hands.

She went out of the back door through the meadow and to the wood. Her legs were shaking. She looked at the tree right on the edge which she always noticed first. It looked down past the meadow towards her cottage. A rowan tree. The sun shone on the ground in front of it and Flora sat down with her back against the tree. Slowly she took the letter out of her pocket to make quite sure she had read those first words correctly. The kitten appeared and curled up on her lap as she unfolded the pages.

Chapter 13

<u>Sybil's First Letter to Flora</u>

Hello, my dear Flora.

Let me introduce myself. I am your Great, Great Aunt Sybil - your real aunt. My younger brother died many years ago. His son who died in a plane crash, was your grandfather.

I expect, unless you have found out the truth before, which I very much doubt, that you will be feeling shocked, confused, and rather angry. Bear with me.

When your grandfather was killed, your grandmother lasted two months before she left all her worldly possessions with me and disappeared forever to 'find herself'. Nothing has been heard of her since. Two of the worldly possessions she left behind with me were her 10-year-old daughter and her 6-month-old baby girl.

I was 63 years old and had never married, therefore had no experience with children. Being left alone to bring up two young girls was an enormous task. In the event, Matilda, the older sister, was a good-mannered, pleasant child, much like her father. We got on well and she helped me to look after Jennet, her younger sister. How I'd have managed without her, I just don't know.

Jennet, on the other hand, was an awkward child. Quick to anger. Matty was the only one who could handle her. I realised it wasn't Jennet's fault and tried to make up for the loss of her father and mother but well, even now in my 96th year, we hardly speak. I blame myself entirely. Actually, I blame her mother but we won't go into that.

We lived in Gallipot Cottage, the family home and my home now, as my nephew had lived in a larger house nearby with his family. Matty loved my cottage. Jennet hated it.

As Matty grew up, she started going out with a local lad. They had been together for two years and had talked about getting married. When she found herself pregnant with you, the wedding was postponed until a later date, Matty liked the idea of you attending as a tiny bridesmaid.

Jennet wasn't happy about a baby taking Matty's attention away from her so she behaved appallingly for a while, even running away from home (taking after her mother) and being brought back by the local postman after we had searched for a full afternoon. She had been hiding in the post office garden shed. Jennet scared herself, I think, as she started to cling to Matty again from then on.

Flora, you will probably be upset about Matilda, your real mother, when you read the next part - and will probably hate me. I hope that you will understand. From what I know of you, I'm sure you will.

Matilda's pregnancy hadn't been straightforward. We knew there were a few problems and I was keeping an eye on her. I trained as a midwife in my young days before I opened the shop but many of the locals called on me if there was anything they needed to know. I successfully delivered many babies in this village. They trusted me and used to send for 'the midwife' as though there was only one.

I have to say here that if there was any risk of complications, I told them beforehand that they must book in at the hospital. Mattie wanted me to deliver her baby, however, in her case I felt she was better off at the hospital and she was booked in there for the birth.

Unfortunately, Matty began to bleed while taking a walk on the moor just behind Pookey Wood. Our wood. Jennet came flying down to fetch me screaming my name. When I reached Matty she had started to give birth - just over a month early. She was in a bad way.

I sent Jennet back to a friend of mine, a Sister at the hospital, who lived in the village. She also had midwife training. I told Jennet to tell Hester to phone for an ambulance and then for her to stay in the house after showing them where we were.

I delivered the baby - you - and you were a tiny little thing. I wasn't sure you would survive. Hester wrapped you up in her coat. It was obvious to us both that Matty was dying. It is a sudden thing that only very rarely happens in pregnancy and believe me when I say nothing could have prevented it.

Your mother held you in her arms, touched her lips to your head and smiled. She whispered 'Her name is

Flora', before she died. I am so sorry Flora. All this must be such a shock for you. What comes next may shock you even more.

I had to calm a distraught Jennet down and then go to the hospital to give details of Matty's death, leaving some details out.... Margaret - Peggy - stayed with her but the incident had left its mark on the child, as it had with all of us. Hester had taken you home a few doors down. She knew how to look after you. Her training was more modern and if anyone could save you, it was her. What I haven't told you is that I had spent the evening, two nights previously, consoling Hester over yet another miscarriage. She was in her forties then and had suffered many miscarriages throughout her life. Her body was tired now and although she desperately wanted a child, she realised that had been her last chance.

We buried your mother's ashes in the wood with a tiny lock of your hair to take with her on her journey. We had taken the chain from her with the 'tree of life' pendant on it, to give to you later in memory of your mother. After a few days, it was obvious that you would live. Hester and Bill took you to her sister for a couple of weeks to avoid questions at the time. People naturally believed the baby had died along with Matty and, for good or bad, we didn't put them right.

Forgive me Flora because at the time, this next action seemed the best thing for you. I still believe that with all my heart.

I went to visit Hester and she asked if she could bring you up as her own child. In the past before the stringent adoption processes of today, this sort of thing was common in close-knit villages. Families took on the babies and children of their friends and other family if they had died or couldn't cope. Now of course it was technically illegal - but also morally right.

I was then 72 years old and had a 9-year-old child to bring up. One that was not only resentful of me but of the baby that she believed had taken her sister away from her. I couldn't cope with a new baby too.

The adoption process would have meant that you would have been in care for quite a while until either adoptive or foster parents were found for you, missing out on the loving care you needed in those early days and which I knew Hester would provide you with. It was helping you and her at the same time.

We agreed that they would move away from the village straight away, to the town where you were brought up and where they had taken you after your birth. As hard as this may seem – they asked me to cease all contact as they were worried I may want you back at some time. I promised her this and a Gardwicke promise made is a promise kept.

I made her promise too. One- that I would leave Gallipot cottage to you when I died. It would have gone to Matty and was yours by rights. Jennet hated the place anyway and wouldn't want it. They could tell you I was a distant great aunt who had no one else to leave it to, as I probably would predecease them.

The second thing was that they had to call you Flora. My promise to Matty. Thirdly, I wanted a phone call every few years to let me know you were well. So there you have it

I have no reason to think this, but I believe you will be taking the news more calmly than most people would. The calmness and the gentleness of your mother perhaps. Please know that you were loved by your real mother and by me, who thought about you every day. But mostly, you were loved so much by Hester and Bill Goode, who may not have been your blood parents but in every other way were your mother and father.

You have an aunt still living in the village, perhaps two because we haven't mentioned your father, have we?

He loved Matty to distraction and when he found out that she had died, he was inconsolable. He flew out of the country the morning after her death and stayed away for many years. His sister didn't know if he was alive or dead for at least three years afterwards. Why didn't he look after you? His sister said he believed you had died along with Matty and as she wasn't sure what had happened at the time, she couldn't put him right.

Which worked out for the best. He couldn't have looked after you. He was out of his mind with grief and, like Jennet, even if it was only at the back of his mind, he might have blamed your birth for her death. I can't say this enough Flora – it was NOT your fault!

He hadn't even felt able to face the burial service. Instead, he buried himself in his work abroad to forget her. I don't know if it worked - but he never married. I am not telling you his name. If you want to find him, you will.

There is more to tell you ...but I think you will have more than enough to think about for a while. The next letter is on a different subject and may raise more questions than it answers. Whenever you feel you are ready, the letter is with Margaret Harker.

All my love, dearest Flora
Sybil xxx

Chapter 14

The letter lay on her lap, returned neatly to its envelope. Flora remained sitting against the tree, her head back against its bark, and let the tears flow unchecked down her cheeks. Tears for the mother she had never known who died so young, the aunt, her mother's sister, who was hurting inside even now - and even for herself. This last was tempered by the knowledge that she had lived the best life she could have and the decisions had been the right ones.

Most of all, she wept for the loss of Sybil. For not having the benefit of her wisdom throughout her life. She did feel that her aunt, her *real* great, great aunt, was still with her and she was grateful for meeting her that one time. She found herself trying to recall some scenes from that meeting so she could live it over again. What she did remember now was that, after she had tried to place a daisy chain around Sybil's neck, the old woman had placed a silver chain around her neck in exchange. How could she have forgotten that? She held on to the 'tree of life' pendant now, which she wore every day - and sobbed again.

She felt rather than heard a presence nearby and she opened her eyes to see Peggy standing between two trees in silence. Freya stretched and with a sidelong glance at the old woman, sauntered off into the woods as Peggy watched it. Flora managed a watery smile.

'You found the letter then?' Peggy remarked.

'You know about it?' Flora frowned.

' I knew it existed but not where it was. You were supposed to find it yourself and then ask to see a second letter, which is in my possession.'

'Which I would like to read as soon as possible'

Peggy paused then came over to lower herself slowly onto a mound of grass near to Flora.

'Sybil said that you ought to wait a while, to let the news of the first letter sink in properly before you attempted the second'

'It's sunk in. It sunk in easily because every word she has written, I feel like I have read before. I haven't of course but it just seems familiar.'

She looked over at Peggy as the old woman nodded sagely.

'Also' she continued, 'with respect, Sybil didn't know how stubborn I could be, although I would hazard a guess that she suspected. Now I know of the other letter's existence, I'm not going to be able to rest until I've read it.'

Peggy's mouth twitched as she accepted this. Then her face became serious again.

'Why did you come out here to read it?' she asked Flora.

'I don't know. I just felt I needed to. Why?'

'No reason.'

'I hate it when people say that. There was obviously a reason.'

Flora sighed and leaned forward, her elbows on her bent knees. Peggy replied with another question.

'Why did you choose *this* tree to sit under?'

'Well I – Ah, now there is definitely a reason behind that question. What is it?'

Peggy hesitated only for a few seconds. Flora needed to know.

'Matty - your mother - her ashes are buried here.'

Flora sprang up as though she had somehow committed sacrilege by sitting there.

'She didn't die here. It was elsewhere in the wood but we scattered her ashes here in view of the cottage, then we planted the rowan tree over them to protect her.'

' I thought rowan trees were meant to protect *against* witches.'

'They are meant to protect against *evil*. We are not evil. The rowan watches over her, the meadow and the cottage.'

The two women held each other's eyes and smiled. With a sudden brisk manner as though she just remembered something, Flora held a hand down towards Peggy.

'Do you want a hand up?'

'I want two hands up if you can spare them.'

Flora prised Peggy from the ground.

'I'll come round for the letter tomorrow if that's all right.'

'Yes of course. Why tomorrow? Why the change of heart?'

'I have something urgent to do. I have to see Jen. I need to talk to her.' and she turned and walked back down through the meadow and the cottage as though she was on a mission.

Peggy had opened her mouth to object but it would make no difference. Flora was a force of nature. She couldn't even let Jennet know as Flora would be almost there now. It was all happening too quickly. The three of them suddenly couldn't keep up. As soon as she had met with Bianca and Jennet at the Folly to discuss the discovery of the Faestone, they knew they were dealing with something special and would have to let events take their course. What would be would be. Flora possibly had more power than Sybil herself. Sybil had been around seventy when she found the stone. Flora had found it on her second night in the village - and had no idea yet what it was.

And the cat… The black kitten with the white streak near one ear. The only photo Peggy had of Sybil was of when she had silver hair, which happened very early in her case. Yet, Peggy remembered her when she was younger with hair as long, as thick and as black as Flora's with one exception. The thin white streak on the right-hand side of her hair

*

This time Jen wasn't behind the counter and so didn't have to bid a hasty retreat on Flora's entrance. Steve looked up and smiled.

'Was the book any good?'

She had found a thin volume of *Starting up your own Internet Business* and whereas it repeated most of what she already knew, she had found a couple of useful tips.

'It was fine thanks. Is Jen in?'

Steve looked wary.

'Yes, I think so. Shall I go upstairs and check?'

That would give Jen a chance to make an excuse, thought Flora.

'No, it's okay. I'll just go up. I need to see her' and with that, she was behind the counter and halfway up the stairs.

Steve only had time to call his wife's name before Flora was face to face with her aunt in the doorway of the sitting room. Jen was blocking her way.

' What do you want?' she asked with obvious hostility.

'Just to talk, Jen. I know now who you are - and who I am - and what happened. *Please*, can we talk?'

'There's nothing to say.'

'Everyone thinks you blame me for my mother's death.'

'Where did you hear–' Jen began.

'But *I* don't' interrupted Flora. 'I don't believe for a minute that you blame me.'

Jen stood, her arms on either side of the doorway, stopping the younger woman from entering - but her expression had changed from belligerence to something like panic.

'It's all right Jen' said Flora in the same soothing voice she had used to calm down the nervous and overwrought Fury. 'I promise you that by the time I leave here, we will have begun the journey to a solid friendship.'

Jen listened to her, searching Flora's face, her brows knitting. What she saw there made her step back and let her niece into the room.

*

They were seated at a table in the window overlooking the street below. She hadn't been offered a drink but she would have refused. Next time perhaps. Jen had resumed the sulky expression.

'What did you mean? And I didn't say I blamed you for her death. Ever.'

'I think it was assumed from your attitude, that's all.'

' How could you possibly know that or know what my attitude was?'

'I can see how it would have been mistaken. You appeared to resent me but it wasn't resentment was it? It was guilt.'

Jen stood up angrily, her hands pressed onto the table.

'Get out! How dare you? I don't want you here. Just GO'

Flora sat calmly. She reached across for Jen's hand but it was withdrawn before contact was made. She spoke quietly.

'I need you to know this. I need you to know that I don't blame you at all. Not even a little.' she said gently.

Jen uttered something between a scream and a sob.

'You don't blame *me*? Oh, that's very good of you. Why the hell should you blame me?'

' I don't. You blame yourself.'

There was an intake of breath from across the table. Then Jen slowly lowered herself into the chair again.

'You blame yourself and I'm not quite sure why. We need to find out and exorcise it. One thing I am sure of is that it wasn't your fault. Not only did Sybil say in a letter that nothing at all could have prevented my mother's death from happening when it did - but I know in my own mind that you had nothing to do with your sister's death. And I know you've been blaming yourself ever since. Letting it poison your life, making you spiky, giving a false impression of the real you - all because of a guilty conscience that you have attached to an innocent soul.'

Jen had ceased to move and, incapable of speech, stared across at this young dark woman, so like Matty. This time when Flora reached forward to hold her hands, there was no movement to stop it. They stayed like that for quite a few seconds. Then sobs wracked the older woman's body and she fell forward onto the table, giving vent to years of hellish torment.

Flora stroked her hand for a while then went quietly to find the kitchen, which was in a back room. After a minute or two and as the sobs diminished to the odd sniffle, she carried two hot cups of tea through. Reaching into her pocket she pulled out a clean tissue. She handed it to the woman with the puffy red face and mascara down her cheeks who took it gratefully with - was that a smile? Flora smiled back just in case.

Jen shifted in her seat. She stared out of the window as she took sips of the steaming tea and then with a last wipe with the tissue, she seemed to make her mind up. She began to speak.

'I wanted to go and collect heather from the moors that day. I'd got it into my mind and my stubborn nature wouldn't let it go. I wasn't allowed to go up on the moors by myself. I was only nine years old but not only that, I was prone to wandering too far away and losing track of time. They had to send the newsagent's lad out looking for me once when dusk was falling. So I was banned.

'I asked Matty if she'd come with me even though I knew she was very pregnant with you. She hadn't been feeling well either. She refused many times until I wore her down. She said she would come with me into the wood and then I could pick the first bunch of heather that I could see on the moor while she watched me. She explained it was too rough for her to walk on the moor in case she tripped.

' I was happy with this and I did find a bunch of heather that was in bloom. But I could see some that was even better a little further out. Then another patch further than that which had more colour than the others. I was in my own selfish little world and only vaguely remembered hearing Matty call my name When it finally registered - only after I'd got the best bunch of heather I could find - I turned back towards her voice.

She was standing, hands on hips, annoyed with me. I had honestly turned back towards her and she wasn't even standing on the moor, only at the edge of the wood. She shook her head at me like she sometimes did when she was just pretending to be annoyed with me. She put her arm out with her 'Come on you rascal' gesture and laughed. She actually laughed! And I grinned back at her. She saw that I had nearly reached her and she turned to walk back then... '

Jen's tears began to flow again and her voice trembled but she carried on.

'She just crumpled up. No cry, nothing. She fell on the floor and rolled over onto her back. I screamed and ran to her. I thought she was dead. She wasn't moving and her eyes were closed. Then her eyelids flickered and she looked up at me and she smiled.'

There was a pause which Flora didn't interrupt, while Jen gathered herself.

'She smiled and said "Don't worry, Jenny Wren. Bring Sybil to me quickly." You probably know the rest.'

Jen gave a long shuddering sigh as though she had experienced a physical pain being removed from her body. She had never confessed this to anyone before today. Flora watched her and knew that what had been removed was the mental burden she had carried around with her nearly all her life. While maybe not disappearing altogether, it might now allow her aunt to live with herself.

She grasped told of Jen's hands and this time felt a firm connection between them both and judging by the uncharacteristically gentle look in Jen's eyes, she felt the same. They held each other's hands tightly, neither willing to let go.

Gradually. Flora felt something else coming through this connection and she frowned. Seeing this, Jen pulled her hands away.

'Is everything all right?' she asked, frowning too.

'I would say everything is going to be perfect.' beamed Flora.

'How can you tell that just from holding hands?'

' I feel that now that you've let go of the guilt that you should never have felt, all the negative feelings have been swept away to make way for something much more positive. I'm sure you will be far happier than ever very soon. Things are working out how you have always wanted them to.'

Jen sighed with relief.

' I don't know why I believe you but I do. You must be powerful.' she whispered in awe.

' Powerful?' laughed Flora, taken aback. 'It's not magic! It's logical that when you let go of feelings that hold you back, good things will happen.'

They hugged with genuine warmth.

As Flora went down the stairs she thought. 'Although there was something I felt when I held her hands which was beyond my comprehension'

As Jen watched her go, she thought 'You can deny it all you like Flora - but how come no one else, even those well versed in the old ways, knew what I was really feeling all these years? You knew exactly.

'And you felt something else. Could it be - after all this time?'

Chapter 15

There was a sound in Flora's ears as she stood on the narrow pavement outside the bookshop. As she had her eyes shut it didn't register what the noise was at first, until she looked up and saw a huge black horse staring down at her. There stood Fury with Cal on his back and Finn running up behind. She took it all in quietly before putting her hands to her face and bursting into tears.

'Well, this is new. I don't usually have such an extreme effect on people, especially as I haven't yet said a word.'

Cal waited calmly for an answer and Flora's tears stopped almost immediately. She wasn't prone to emotional outbursts but she still felt embarrassed. Today seemed a day of non-stop tears from her and Jen.

'It's not you and they're happy tears. Or at least tears of relief.'

'Glad to hear it. I was on my way to see you again to ask if you wanted to come for lunch and have a roam around the moors. To see if you can find the stones you sheltered under? I'm guessing this isn't a good time?'

Flora stroked Fury's muzzle whilst stroking the top of Finn's head at the same time.

'You know what? I think this is the perfect time.'

'So it takes your mind off other things?

'Exactly,'

'That's all right. I don't mind being used as an emotional support.'

'Good. I don't mind being used as a moorland guide either.'

They laughed easily together and after Cal dismounted, all four of them walked up towards the lane opposite the inn. They reached the end of the lane and viewed moorland as far as they could see, with no sign of Cal's farmhouse or of the mysterious disappearing stones.

'If you were a gentleman, you'd let me ride on Fury's back to the farmhouse' she teased.

'It's because I'm a gentleman that I won't. He won't have anyone on his back but me and he's prone to throwing people off. Especially me when I first rescued him.'

'I think I'll be okay. I know stroking him isn't the same as being in the saddle but...' she tailed off. 'You rescued him?'

'Yes, when I came here. Finn was rescued too, six weeks before that. I still think we chose each other. They had both been badly treated and the rehoming centres thought that a farmhouse in the middle of nowhere was the perfect home for two such nervous animals.'

'You've done a good job with them.' Flora told him with genuine warmth. 'If you can bring them amongst villagers like you did today. You've made good progress at socialising them.'

'There's still a long way to go' he said, gratefully receiving the compliment. 'For instance, young slender women wouldn't be able to keep control of Fury.'

Flora didn't say anything but her eyes pleaded with him.

'On your own head be it' Cal sighed, giving in, 'and I hope that doesn't turn out to be physically true.'

Flora gently talked to the stallion as Cal shortened the stirrups. She took her time getting hold of the reins, letting him get used to her touch on the withers. Then slowly carefully, she hoisted herself up using Cal's hand as a mounting step and sat still and quiet. talking to him all the time. He danced about from side to side for a minute but only gently, more as a token rebellion. Eventually, she squeezed his sides almost imperceptibly while keeping a firm hand on the reins and let him walk forward at his own pace. He seemed perfectly happy. She chanced a smug smile in Cal's direction. He shook his head.

'I'm speechless' he said.

'So am I. I haven't been horse riding since I left school and it's a long, long way up here.'

'Serves you right' Cal grinned

They walked on in companionable silence for a few minutes and then he asked about her uncharacteristic show of tears and why it had happened. After her explanation during which he kept silent, he was astounded.

'You move here not knowing that you're properly related to anyone. Only to find out that you have an aunt living almost next door and a great couple of times aunt who left you the family cottage - and are related to most of the earlier inhabitants. too? I'm glad you've made up with the virago at the bookshop. I'm sorry you never met Sybil again by the way.

' I think you'll find she is no longer a virago. And thank you. Did you know Sybil?'

'We crossed paths quite a few times. Put it this way, if you thought Jen Cayley was a prickly customer then it's maybe as well you didn't meet Sybil. At least in her later years.'

'That doesn't sound like her. Did you rub her up the wrong way?'

Cal put his head down.

'May have done' he muttered.

'Ha' said Flora with relish.

'Only because I wanted to write about the Witches of Farstone and she point blank refused even though she knew I was sympathetic to the Old Ways. She used to say "You won't understand so I'll save myself the bother". For heaven's sake. It's what I do for a living. You can't write successful books unless you understand your subject.'

He watched Flora laugh as she thought of her Aunt Sybil giving him the cold shoulder and a thought suddenly occurred to him.

'Although now you are a Gardwicke instead of a Goode and your ancestry is the same one that preceded Sybil through the centuries, perhaps you could help?'

He looked up at her with a puppy dog expression, no doubt learnt from Finn.

'I don't know anything about my ancestry' she said, being economical with the truth. She suddenly grinned. 'Anyway, you wouldn't understand so I'll save myself the bother.'

*

Cal had called at the farmhouse and collected a picnic he had prepared. He had left Fury happily turned out in the paddock behind the barn but Finn had accompanied them up onto the moor above the farmhouse. They had wandered the moor around that area, up and down hills with Flora turning back to try and view the farmhouse at every point. There was nothing to see. They had walked every inch of the moor where it was still possible to view Cal's home and there was nothing.

Flora was beginning to believe she had imagined the whole thing - but how could she have? The stones had kept most of the deluge of rain from her. It had given her shelter, respite against the storm. Without it, she may not have survived. So where was it?

Frustrated, both she and Cal gave up their fruitless search and settled down near a spring which tumbled over limestone and disappeared underground. Cal put the basket on the ground and Flora helped herself to sandwiches, chicken legs, apples and tea from a flask. They sat in silence until Flora ventured an opinion.

'This is completely weird. What the hell is going on? I can remember exactly the position I was in when I saw the light from your farmhouse. It was sort of in a diagonal line from here. I remember finding the stones almost as if they had just appeared there. I didn't think about it. I was just so happy to find somewhere to shelter. I thought I was going to die before that.'

Cal smiled and shook his head.

'You're not going crazy. I honestly believe you may have seen the Faegate or the Faestone.

'The one that Farstone is named after?' interrupted Flora. 'Well, if it's named after it, it must exist. It must be around here somewhere. Below a bluff? Hiding in a little valley?'

'Was it hiding when you saw it?'

'No, it was just on - or perhaps just below - the crest of a hill which looked down on your farmhouse?'

Cal frowned.

' Describe it' he said.

'Like I said, it was - what did I call it before? A dolmen? There were two upright stones with a large flat stone propped across them. A capstone? There was a short tunnel formed by the stones, going through it.'

He looked up.

'Tunnel? Not a chamber going underground?'

'Like a burial chamber, you mean? No, it was dark but I could see what looked like a stormy sky through it at the other end or, maybe more like a whirlwind twisting round, moving the air.'

She reflected on this, unaware of how still Cal had become. She hadn't really thought about it before - but now she remembered the feeling she had when she looked into that dark maelstrom.

'I didn't want to go further on through the passage the stones made, even though it might have given me more protection from the rain if I had. I just felt I should stay where I was on the edge of the shelter. Weird...' she mused, her brows lowered.

After a few seconds, she became aware of Cal's silence. She raised her head towards him. His black eyes pierced hers.

'You didn't want to go any further because you had found the Faery portal into their world.

That is what the Faestone is. Your remarkable instincts stopped you from going through the portal to risk being lost forever in their world.'

Flora stared back at him in disbelief. It was all she could do not to burst out laughing.

'Surely you can't believe that? You sound like the Storyteller at the inn. It's just one of your folklore stories. A tale from long ago when things like that seemed real to people because they didn't know any better.'

Cal was angry. His mouth was set and his jaw twitched.

' And you think we know better now, do you? You think that science and technology can explain everything, do you? That the new ways are best and the old ways were the product of ignorant people who knew no better?'

He spat these last words out.

'Oh, come on.' Flora could feel her temper rising too. 'Surely you can't believe the stones were a portal into another world, peopled by beings we cannot confirm the existence of?'

'Confirm the existence of? Why do things always have to be proved? Can't you have a little faith? That is what the modern world has done to us - wanting proof for everything and even when they have that proof, not believing it. The world has lost touch with what it once was and we are so much the poorer for it. If you want proof of the existence of this portal then you will have to find it first. And as you have searched the moor where you swore it was, we have another dilemma, don't we? Because if it isn't where you said it was, did it exist? Did you make it up? And if you were telling me the truth about this place that doesn't exist... then I will have to take my own leap of faith to believe you, won't I?'

He unclenched his fists and rubbed his face hard with both hands. He went on speaking more quietly.

'The Faestone is very rarely seen. It is seen only when it is needed and only to certain people. It may have existed here on the moors for eternity, but for all but the chosen few, it remains invisible. Unfortunately, I don't seem to be one of the chosen few.'

Flora couldn't trust herself to say anything. From wanting to make fun of his theory, there was something in him now that made her believe him. What he said, had started to make sense to her. Was this place making her crazy? Had she been wrong to move here? Yet -where were the stones? How could she deny their existence when she had seen them, felt them, sheltered inside them?

'I'm sorry, I don't know where it is but it did exist, I know that so…'

She tailed off. It was all she could offer. The way the day had turned out meant an end to the pleasantries. Cal shoved the remains of the picnic back in the basket and they made their way, in silence, back in the direction of the farmhouse. Neither one wanted to make things any worse by referring to their conversation, but neither could they force any small talk from themselves.

As they reached the farmhouse, Flora managed a, 'Thank you for the picnic'. Cal managed. 'Will you be okay walking back?' and that was it. As Flora set off at a rapid pace towards the village she turned back. Cal was nowhere to be seen but Finn stood there looking straight in her direction with the saddest expression on his face, before disappearing from sight.

Flora wanted to cry for the third time that day. She just needed to get home to Gallipot Cottage, attack a bottle of wine with intent and put the whole strange day behind her. When she opened the door she found a letter on the doormat, addressed to her in Sybil's hand. Peggy hadn't waited, she had posted it through already.

Flora squeezed her eyes shut and let a shuddering sigh escape. Would this make things better - or a whole lot worse?

Chapter 16

<u>Sybil's second letter to Flora</u>

Hello again dearest Flora,

I hope by now you are coming to terms with your ancestry. I have no doubt that Hester and Bill kept even a whiff of this from you. It was for your own protection and I completely agreed with them.

As the saying goes, you're a big girl now and you deserve to know who your blood relations are, especially as you will be living in their village. When I say 'their', it is more true than you might think.

The Gardwickes, of which you are one, the Peverels and the Harkers are the oldest families in this village. They have all been here constantly since the time of Hilde, our ancestor in Anglo-Saxon times and other ancestors possibly well before that. Neolithic remains have been found that indicate the constant presence of a community or settlement here since at least that time.

The Gardwicke story starts with Hilde. That would have been her only name at that time, but it would have been qualified by a word or two describing her. For example, Alfred the Potter or Edwin the Farmer. Hilde was Hilde the Geard Wicce. Geard was a garden or enclosure such as the wildflower meadow and Wicce simply meant 'wise woman'. Over time this became the regular surname we use now- Gardwicke.

As the wise woman of the village, she was both healer and midwife. Her cures came out of her garden from the herbs and flowers she grew there. Her potions and medicines were passed down through the years, at first through the oral tradition. You will see them written down at a much later date – remembered by generations afterwards - in the earlier pages of the large leather journal on the shelf, along with later entries. I hope you make good use of it.

She was one of the most respected people in the community. There are records of her in the Peverel's archives. Among other historical accounts, it has her acquiring a large parcel of land behind her cottage. Or rather exchanging the land for being on call whenever any of the Peverel family were ill or with child, giving her services for free. You will probably see where this is going.

Yes, that parcel of land is now the wildflower meadow behind our cottage. Gallipot cottage has been lived in by members of the Gardwicke family since Hilde's time even though it has had a few transformations. You can see now why I wanted it to stay in the family, can't you?

Unfortunately, as things are today, women don't always want to settle down with families. I didn't myself, but as long as there is Gardwicke blood here, then I feel that my job is done. You are a true Gardwicke. Now I should explain what that means in reality and that is the most difficult part. Perhaps not as difficult as the revelation in my first letter but still tough to grasp.

As I said, wicce meant 'wise woman', a healer and later – 'witch'. There were other women trained by Hilde who became wise women. As the village grew, the number of wise women who were taught the old ways was over-proportionate to the population here. That's why Farstone became known, even centuries ago, as the village of Witches.

At the beginning of the 1600s, Sir Ralph Peverel rebuilt all the cottages of the village with new, strong building materials and they have survived as such today. I say this to show you how the Peverels were unusual in that they were good to the residents of their village and in return received both the loyalty and the labour of the villages.

Not long after came the Witch Trials. The persecutors came to Farstone, whose reputation had preceded it. Any wicce or indeed any woman they could find was herded into the street. They were tied up to wait for the carts to arrive to carry them to the city for trial, as if they would ever receive a fair one. Sir Ralph jumped in to save them. He had good reason. His daughter was among the witches spread in the dust of the street.

He persuaded the men, with the aid of rather a large sum of money, that he was a personal friend of the king and that these wholly innocent women were under his protection. He could vouch for them as they were ordinary women who did no magic. Because of this, the despicable witch trials left Farstone unscathed.

What he said wasn't quite true though. Magic did touch just a few of the women. None more so than the Gardwickes. Not a malevolent, evil kind of magic, but a gentle type of magic.

I can't speak for the other families as it is not my place but as for the Gardwickes, their powers of healing were so much stronger because of the power behind the thought. They didn't just put a poultice on or deliver a dose of physic down a person's throat. They <u>willed</u> it to work. They could feel in their minds if it would work and the touch of their hands was the best healing medicine that could be imagined. Their patients swore they could feel heat coming from their fingertips. I feel the same when I heal, thoughts and hopes go into the healing. I know I have delivered or saved babies that should have died. I have healed burns that shouldn't have healed. I have tunnelled into minds and found what really ailed them

Many times it's not just the body that needs healing but the mind. In many cases when people took to their bed with no reason and weakened themselves, you had to heal the mind first in order to heal the body. It's a process we in Farstone simply know as Empathy. Available to all but in practice, very rarely used to its full capacity.

It seems to be hardwired into the collective Gardwicke brain. Your mother Matilda would have been a powerful Wicce. I think you are very much like her. This is where you come in.

I broke my promise to Hester and Bill when you were seven years old. I had promised to leave you completely alone, but I had this feeling that I needed to see you. Seven is an important age for a wicce. They start to develop their potential at that age. The capabilities become apparent to those who know. Hester and Bill wouldn't have known how to recognise it and I felt like I needed to be there with you, to see if you were displaying any of the signs that nature not nurture was taking its course in you.

What I found in the short time I spent with you was that the Gardwicke inheritance was in safe hands, should you choose to take on the mantle. I felt sure that you would.

The thing that convinced me most of all was your empathy for the flowers and trees in your garden. If you have empathy for natural things, you have empathy for everything. You may not remember how you talked to me of the sound of the trees rustling. How you handled, the flowers so delicately. How you picked some daisies for me and made me a daisy chain. You laughed when it wouldn't go over my head so I put it over yours instead. Then I added another chain, do you remember? It belonged to your mother, given to her by her father on her last birthday before he was killed. It was very precious to her. This was her 'Tree of Life' necklace.

You were, according to Bill, the only one who could calm the slavering beast next door. The dog was just like putty in your hands. You were obviously letting it know in your mind that you loved it and were no threat. With these things and the fact that you had melted the heart of this crabby old woman, I knew that the empathy you had for all living things was your strength. You have no idea how happy that visit made me and it has cemented the future of the Gardwickes, at least for the time being.

So, my dear Flora, you find yourself a Gardwicke in Farstone, the village of witches. There are more of us here than you think. It is your rightful place and the continuation of a long tradition. I don't want you to feel like you are trapped in a cage, so if you feel like this, you must leave. I suspect that you will stay.

Are we witches? I will leave you to make your own interpretation of this. What is a witch? Certainly not the fairy tale warty witch, the old crone who cast evil spells on their enemies and rode on a broomstick. Certainly not the poor women who were killed in the 17th century on false pretences cooked up by corrupt men on a mission and by jealous women.

Today's witch, if we have to label her so, is a power for good. She may just follow the rules of nature or have knowledge of the craft through study. Sometimes the study will reveal a certain natural skill set. She may find she has a talent or, dare I say power, in some of the forms associated with us. Divination, healing, mediumship, and natural psychic abilities amongst others. If we have to be called anything instead of these processes being accepted as one aspect of normal, then a witch is as good as anything.

Of course, it has bad connotations too, but think of the name as honouring all those people who were called witches in the past and died for it. You can choose to take up this mantle or not. I think it may have already chosen you.

There is one more thing which I must mention. Something that takes us into other realms and for which you may now, possibly rightly, regard me as a mad old woman. I don't think this will ever touch you, but in case it does, I need you to be aware.

Long ago The witches of Farstone were associated with the Fae. They were the only people around here whom the Fae would communicate with, according to legend, This legend hasn't come alive for many generations - but then the Fae don't have normal lifespans according to any knowledge we have of them.

If you think about it, the village name itself was based on the legend of the Faery Stone, Faestone, now known as Farstone. The stone was somewhere on Farstone Moor above the village and was supposed to be a portal into the world of the Fae.

Legend had it that any human who passed through this portal would be lost forever. It was used by the Fae to leave their changelings on when they had stolen human babies in their place. All just legend you may think and should stay as such. Those were my thoughts exactly when I was young except for two things.

One, I know one of the Fae. I base this on the fact that he has not aged in the whole time he has visited our realm. I don't know, I can only believe the evidence of my own eyes and Culhain is that evidence. Alongside this agelessness, he knows things he can't possibly know. Peggy is the person who can feel their presence more than I can and understands them more.

The second thing is that, here in Farstone, we still believe in fairies. Please don't laugh, you may find yourself believing the same. Pookey

Wood, which you own, is named after the mischievous sprites that were supposed to live there. Puck, Puca, pixies, whatever you want to call them. They were shape-shifters and although I have felt nothing but a good atmosphere in the woods, this was what the people in much earlier times named it.

Somewhere on Farstone Moor, the Faestone, their portal into the realm of the Fae doesn't exist for most people. It is a legend, a myth. Yet I know for a fact that both my mother and grandmother each saw it once in their lives at least. I too have seen it once when I urgently needed to find it. I felt as though the Fae made it appear for me when I was in need. Perhaps because in this village, we still believe.

So it does exist. Whether or not you will be able to see it yourself and furnish yourself with proof, I have no idea.

Perhaps like us, you will only find it once when you are in need of it.

I apologise again for telling you about the Witches of Farstone and expecting you to accept it. I think that you will believe, eventually at least and realise that you are one of us. I also apologise for introducing the subject of the Fae, which I never intended to do. Perhaps I wanted to get it all over with at once. Now from thinking me a mildly eccentric but harmless old woman, you will think me a crazy old crone who should have been locked up years ago.

Whatever else you think, please think of me as your loving aunt who welcomes you, if posthumously, to the family, who will always watch over you and who wishes you every good wish for your life in Farstone.

Your loving aunt,
Sibyl.
xxx

Chapter 17

The wind whistled down the chimney, rattling the window frames as the rain beat against the windows and doors. Flora finished her slice of toast and sat back in the old chair next to the kitchen range with a cup of tea.

She had planned to work in the wildflower meadow, picking some while they were ripe and others as the blooms had started to dry off, depending on their type. She would leave them to dry out, upside down from the beams in her kitchen.

Others, she would leave in the meadow for them to spread their seeds naturally. She was looking forward to trying out a new tea of Herb Robert mixed with Lemon Balm, the latter to neutralise the bitter taste a little. She had found it in Sybil's leather journal. There were new and intriguing recipes, brews and tonics with every page she turned. She had found another use for Herb Roberts as an insect repellent. She just had to check and make sure that she didn't use anything that had now been found to have adverse effects. Strangely, for such ancient recipes, these were few and far between. The Gardwickes knew their stuff.

To paraphrase Charlotte Bronte, 'There was no possibility of taking a walk in the meadow today', so here she was, relaxing for a change. She sipped her tea and decided not to waste the day. She would go into Beck Isle town and pick up the flyers and posters she had ordered. She needed to get her village business 'out there' now.

The online one was doing very well and took up most of her time at the moment but she wanted something local, to give something back to them. She had changed the name of the shop from her earlier idea of 'Natural Healing' It seemed too boring now after all she had learned and she had to think of something quickly for the posters. She hoped she had made the right decision.

She leaned back in Sybil's fireside chair and put her head against the old but carefully cleaned, embroidered cushion. She was still trying to feel something about the second of Sybil's letters. It was over a month now since she had read it- read both of the letters – and she felt that she should have been far more shocked than she was. Of course, there had been indications of things going this way.

If she was honest, the letter had only confirmed what she already suspected. It *was* a famous village of witches after all. The family she now knew she belonged to were prominent in the art of healing. Sybil had already been known as the Wildflower Witch. The surprise had been that she herself was thought of as a witch by Sybil, not only because of the Gardwicke tradition but because of what she had discovered when Flora was 7 years old.

If she hadn't moved here, if she hadn't chosen the profession she was in, if Sybil hadn't left her the cottage or written those letters… then she might not feel as 'different' as she now did. There were more 'ifs'. If she hadn't felt kinship with animals throughout her life, if she hadn't been able to look deep into people's minds – a recent thing. If she hadn't seen that damn Faestone. What on earth was that all about?

There was one thing she knew, she had been wrong to make fun of and to get annoyed with

Cal. She owed him an apology and she knew she would have to swallow her pride. What he said and what he thought was exactly the same as Sybil's beliefs. Folklore was his whole life and she had dismissed it out of hand. How would she feel if someone told her that her healing was a load of superstitious nonsense and she ought to live in the real world? Unfortunately, when she had trekked out to his farmhouse a few days later to eat humble pie, all three of the inhabitants were out. Then when she was about to try again, Mary said her mum Philippa – who knew everything that went on in the village – said he was in London, seeing his publishers. The local vet's assistant was looking after the animals for a few days, as he usually did.

Flora felt hurt that he hadn't asked her to watch over them but why should he let a relative stranger stay in his home anyway, even if the relative stranger *hadn't* had a row with him in the middle of the moor? She had given up trying to contact him after that. He probably wanted nothing more to do with her.

She had reflected long and hard on his words, especially the parts about the new world losing touch with the old. Perhaps she should have a little faith after all. This was her world now and more and more, she was beginning to believe she belonged to it. Although there were lots of questions she needed answers to. Braving the heavy rain, she got into the car and drove towards Beck Isle.

*

Beck Isle was deserted. It was usually heaving in the early summer but this deluge was putting people off from doing their shopping. She easily found a parking space right in the market square. She had just started to walk up the steep main street towards the stationer's shop when she noticed a four-track at the side of the road. It looked familiar and was definitely recognisable when the two occupants got out. One was a taller-than-average, black-haired man with a nice line in designer stubble and macho swaggers. She moved quickly to the side and took shelter in the arched stone entrance to a flea market. She stood with her feet in a large puddle wondering why on earth she was hiding from Cal.

Unfortunately, the other occupant of the car had been Finn and Flora hadn't moved quickly enough to escape his notice. She only got the warning a couple of seconds before, as Cal's voice shouted 'Finn. Come HERE!'

The next moment, a huge shadow appeared in front of her as Finn, big enough normally, stood on his hind legs and, putting his paws on Flora's shoulders, proceeded to lick her face. It was totally unexpected so she lost her balance, teetered back with Finn jumping about as though it was a game – and sat heavily in the middle of the dirty puddle.

Cal, who had arrived in time to see it all, tried to call Finn away but couldn't get the sound out as he was laughing too much. So, consequently, Finn thought everyone was having fun and put his paws on Flora's shoulders yet again, this time making her fall flat on the floor, her hair trailing in the puddle, while Finn tried to lick the mud off her nose with glee.

'Finn' came a weak and not at all commanding voice because the speaker was still doubled up, tears rolling down his face. At least it distracted Finn for a moment while Flora tried to scramble up. Cal came over to offer his hand which she reluctantly took in case Finn wanted to 'play' again.

'Are you alright' he spluttered, looking anything but concerned.

'Do I look alright?' she shot back.

He looked at her. She couldn't have been much wetter if she'd gone for a fully clothed wild swim in the river. Was being soaking wet her 'go-to' appearance? Her hair was in rat's tails, her face streaked with mud from Finn's nose, her clothes were dripping all over and she had a giant, muddy paw mark on each shoulder.

'Oh my god' whimpered Cal, unable to speak yet again through a fresh gale of laughter. He wiped his eyes and tried to collect himself as Finn barked at his own reflection in the puddle. 'I'm so sorry'

'If that's you being sorry' rasped Flora, then I'd hate to see you when you didn't give a damn.'

Cal stood up straight and tried to be serious.

'I think Finn just got carried away. You haven't been to see us in a while and…I think he must have missed you.' Cal started to become sober.

Flora melted a bit.

'I don't blame Finn at all.'

'Do you blame *me*?' he asked with a startled expression.

'Of course not, how can I blame you? If anything it was my fault for standing in a puddle in the first place.'

There was a pause.

'Why were you standing in a puddle?'

'Don't ask. Anyway, I have been up to see you, you were all out. And then I was coming to see you another time but Philippa said you were in London at your publishers?'

He nodded.

'It would have been nice to see you' he said.

'Really? I thought you would have been mad with me. I was coming up to apologise.'

'No, absolutely not, I should be apologising to you. I behaved like a spoilt child.'

'You didn't. Or if you did, then we both did. I wanted to say that, I thought about what you said and I am really trying to have a bit more faith now – for various reasons. Sybil left me a letter that basically agreed with a lot of the things you had said on the moors.'

'It's done now anyway – and I hope we can still be friends.'

'Of course, we *are* friends'

'Finn obviously thinks you're his friend...' he said before a smirk crossed his face.

This reminded first Flora, then Cal, that she was still standing there, dripping wet and being given strange looks by the few passers-by on the street.

'Come on, let's get you somewhere warm and dry. There's a good pub a couple of doors away that does nice food.'

Flora looked down at her clothes and spread her arms out.

'Looking like this?' she asked. He squeezed her shoulder, carefully avoiding the pawmark, and smiled down at her.

'Your clothes under your coat should be dry enough if you take it off – and you can avail yourself of the hairdryer in the loos?'

Flora agreed as there didn't seem any other solution and all three of them entered the pub to a sea of incredulous faces, who watched the Gothic hero, the giant dog and the soaking wet scarecrow walk towards the bar.

*

Cal put Flora's coat over the back of the chair near the fire. It was always lit on grey days to give a cosy atmosphere. By the time they had eaten their meal of steak pie, mash and gravy, the coat was at least half-dry. They had both apologised to each other and Flora had rashly invited him round for Sunday lunch, knowing that roast dinners weren't her forte. Anything you could throw in one large pot and heat up, she was happy with but anything else... She laughed at that last thought. She *was* a witch! Using one pot or a cauldron must be in her blood. Cal looked at her curiously. She answered the look by saying that one day perhaps, she might let him read Sybil's second letter when all would be made clear. But not yet.

They both walked up to the stationers together, Finn keeping close by. As Cal got his supplies, Flora collected her posters and flyers. She held up one of the posters as he walked towards her.

'Well,' he said, inspecting it 'that will certainly get people visiting the shop, even for curiosity's sake alone!'

Chapter 18

There was a knock at the side door and Peggy stood there holding on to the door frame. The rain that had been present for the last couple of weeks had stopped but the winds had increased, especially in the wind tunnel that was Flora's driveway.

Peggy waved aside the invitation to go in the kitchen.

'I thought that perhaps you might want to discuss everything you've learnt. Make some sense of it?'

'It's beginning to make more sense than I ever thought possible. Aren't you coming in then?'

'No, there are more of us. We thought we should have a gathering–'

'As in a coven?' Flora raised her eyebrows. She must try and rid herself of this cynicism as even she was starting to believe it was all possible.

'Whatever you want to call it. We gather. It's a gathering. A Meet. Whatever. Are you coming?'

'Well, yes I suppose so. Where is it?'

'The Folly in the grounds of Peverel Hall. It's where we always meet.'

' Or gather' grinned Flora.

'You're not too old for a clip around the ear' said. Peggy, deadpan.

'I'd better get my coat on then and a woolly hat too. It looks nasty out there.'

'Soft gale blowing' nodded Peggy.

While Flora was working out what a soft gale was, she dressed for the weather and locked up. As they reached the front of the cottage, Jen was walking towards them.

'Blessed be Jennet' said Peggy.

'Blessed be to you both' replied Jen grabbing hold of one of Peggy's arms to keep the old woman upright against the gusts.

As Peggy watched, Flora did an odd thing. Instead of grabbing hold of Peggy's other arm to help Jen keep her upright, she went to the other side of Jen and grabbed her arm instead. Peggy, looked on with amazement as Jen turned to Flora, her eyes wide with surprise and her mouth forming an uncharacteristic smile. Even more surprising to the old woman was that, with an almost imperceptible nod, Jen squeezed her niece in a gesture of great affection. Surely not in such a short time, thought Peggy? Surely they can't have reached this stage from a point of deep antagonism on Jennet's side not too long before? All three of them. Jen in the middle continued up the road, past the newsagent and the Peverel Arms and entered the gateway of Peverel Hall.

*

'Merry Meet'

They all greeted each other with these words as they joined Binky in the Hall's Folly. Flora joined in. It seemed natural. But there were four of them now. She put this into words.

'Am I okay to join you? There won't be three anymore.'

A high-pitched giggle escaped from Binky while the familiar wheeze, which passed for a laugh with Peggy, could be heard next to Flora's ear.

'What do you think we are? The Wyrd sisters from Macbeth? she spluttered.

'Hubble bubble. toil and trouble' sang Binky in a convincing cackle.

'It's double, double, toil–' began Jen and was ignored.

'Sit down Flora' said Peggy.

Feeling slightly miffed and a little silly, Flora did as she was told, taking one of the chairs placed around the central table. Peggy began.

'Now that you've read Sybil's letters and have had time to take them in, are there any questions you want to ask us? We will do our best to answer.'

'I'm sure there are plenty but they're all gone out of my head for the moment. Let me think.'

There was a silence while they all looked at her intently, which didn't help her thought processes.

'Okay,' she said at last, 'let's start with the first letter. I now know that you are my aunt, Jen and I'm very happy to have discovered this. I didn't know I had any living relatives so to find you living almost next door is unbelievable.'

She stretched forward to grab Jen's hands again. While Jen squeezed hard and grinned, Binky who had no idea of this turn of events, let out a little 'mmff' noise of surprise and wondered who this pleasant, happy person formerly known as Jennet was. Peggy looked on in wonder. What magic had Flora worked when she visited her aunt that day?

'Although' Flora went on, 'Sybil mentioned the possibility of two aunts?'

Binky giggled.

'That might be me' she said happily. 'No, that is definitely me.'

'Bianca' Peggy said sternly. 'You don't know that for sure. You can't get her hopes up like that.'

'I *do* know for sure' Binky shot back defensively.

Peggy lowered her head and pierced Binky's skull with her best withering look.

'How?' she asked.

'Oh Peggy, you can be so old-fashioned sometimes. Well, you know I've met Flora a couple of times? I just happened to brush her hair from her shoulder at the inn once, in an affectionate gesture of course. And I just happened to keep both of the hairs as they somehow found their way into a clean handkerchief. Then I sent them up with one of my hairs and one of Ralph's hairs from a jacket in his wardrobe. He was last here over 2 years ago and I was worried the hair was too old as I don't know how these things work. So I sent mine up too, to make sure.

'Too old for what?' Peggy scowled.

'Why, DNA testing of course.' Binky smiled innocently, unaware of the bombshell she was dropping, 'and it came back as proof positive we were all very closely related and there was little doubt that Ralph was Flora's father.'

She sat back and beamed. Flora leant forward.

'And that is definite?'

Peggy closed her eyes.

'Yes. I can show you the results. I'm the other aunt that Sybil mentioned' she cleared her throat as her voice had suddenly gone squeaky 'and well, my brother Ralph is your father.'

There was a different kind of wheeze as Peggy let out the breath she didn't realise she had been holding. Jen came around the table to put her arm around Flora who sat with both hands covering her face. Binky sat in an abashed silence, only now becoming aware that maybe she should have approached this without hobnail boots on.

Flora dropped her hands and looked around at the stricken faces of the other three. Suddenly she wanted to laugh. It obviously wasn't the reaction they would be expecting so she resisted the impulse and smiled at them instead.

'There's one thing I can say. My life since I moved here has been anything but boring.'

Chapter 19

The relief felt by the women of the Folly was almost tangible. Binky had been close to tears and gulped now while trying to smile at the same time. Flora went to the head of the table to give her a hug.

'I'm so glad I've found another relative. Two aunts, no less. So, yes it's all a shock but strangely, not as much as it should have been. I feel quite content with it all. A little bit apart perhaps, like it's happening to someone else and not me.'

Happy tears sprung to Binky's eyes.

'Oh, I'm so relieved. I thought you were going to hate me forever for a minute.

Flora laughed and then said,

'Perhaps the conversation about my father could be had at another time. I feel like I've had enough revelations just recently to last me a lifetime.'

'Of course' said Binky, grasping at the chance of not having to explain all about her brother just yet. 'You must come round to Peverel Hall for afternoon tea when you're ready then maybe I can try and explain.'

'I will' Flora replied, then she turned to Peggy.

' And you, Peggy. You've been like another close relative to me ever since I arrived here. Can I claim you as another aunt even if we're not related by blood?'

Peggy coloured up. It was the first time Flora had seen her looking embarrassed but her eyes twinkled and she looked extremely pleased.

'I think I'd like that' she said, ' I can't take Sybil's place but I can deputise for her.'

' Fantastic' said Flora 'three aunts.'

Then her face broke into a wicked grin.

'You really will be the three witches from Macbeth now. I can call you the Wyrd Aunts.'

'Don't push it' said Peggy as Binky laughed and Jen waved her arms in the air in a depiction of an evil witch over a cauldron.

'You're the fourth' Jen reminded Flora 'as Sybil was. Are you comfortable with that?'

'Ah. Now we come to the second letter' replied Flora as they all took their places around the table again.

'I don't think there will be any revelations this time' Peggy said glancing at a cowed Binky because I think Sybil will have covered most of it, but is there anything you need to know?'

'Again, I am sure there will be many, many things I need to ask as time goes on but as for now… I have thought about it ever since I found out about my ancestry.'

'Do you think of yourself as a witch?' Peggy encouraged her, 'What does being a witch mean to you?'

There was a long pause then Flora stood up.

'Just give me five minutes for a little fresh air and to gather my thoughts.'

They all nodded in recognition of this and Flora stepped out onto the terrace and then onto the grass beside the Folly, needing to be amongst the trees that hid it from the Hall. Their leaves blew in the strong wind, sounding like it was another language of their own.

What *did* it mean to her? How could she answer this when she hadn't made sense of it fully, in the time since she'd found it out? Would she consider herself a witch or a healer or were they both the same? Were her healing powers achieved through the herbs and flowers she used? Or was there something more as well?

Flora leant against the tree for support - emotional rather than physical - and felt her head was reeling, spinning, - one thought chasing another in never-ending circles. Perhaps it had been too much to take in all at once. The move to Farstone, the business start-up, one revelatory letter, then another, Cal and the Faestone legend and the possibility that she had found it….

She closed her eyes and slid down the trunk, trying to clear her mind as she sat there. She thought of sitting against her mum's rowan tree and tried to picture her. She hadn't seen any photographs of her yet, they weren't a family for recording things on camera but she realised from others reactions how much she must look like her. She would use that to conjure her up in her mind.

'Hello Mum' she whispered 'It's Flora. I'm sorry I never knew you but I feel that you're with me. You're in my blood and now in my thoughts. I love you, Mum.' She gave a little sniffle, drew her arm across her eyes then concentrated again. 'Can you guide me? I don't want to let you or the others down but although I'm happy enough with what we are, I'm also confused. Can you help me, mum? Make it clearer?'

Keeping her eyes closed, she opened her mind.

*

All three of the Wyrd Aunts turned around with concern on their faces as Flora opened the Folly door. She took her place at the table, gave them a reassuring smile and started to speak.

'Just hear me out, please. You asked if I thought of myself as a witch and what it meant to me if I did. I have had time, during the evenings – and often in the middle of the night – to try and come to a conclusion. I have found that I am still confused but – less so just at this moment – so here goes.

'Before I came here, my healing was done through the power of the herbs I used and now the wildflowers I use from the meadow. I still believe that this sort of healing comes primarily from Nature, which has a remedy for everything. This was my training as a herbalist and a healer. Although perhaps, through me, like Sybil, the care and intention used in preparing these remedies might work slightly more than is usual. I do get very good results. Nevertheless, it is something that everyone can do and everyone should make use of. If they feel that extra quality that aids healing, then that is all to the good.'

She looked around the table as they nodded waiting for the 'but'.

'However, I do acknowledge that I have some sort of affinity with animals. I have always known it but recent events at Cal's farmhouse have shown me that there is more behind it than I first thought. For instance, that is not something that can be learnt. It is something that is felt inside and not everyone has it - or at least knows how to use it.

'To show how important this recent revelation has been to me. I have decided to give advice on – and try and heal or calm - not only humans but animals too. Being here has taught me that this gift means something. It means I should use it for the good of other living things.'

She stopped and looked at Jen. There was another 'however' coming.

'However, I have learned since I've been here that maybe, just maybe, I have this gift with humans too. Perhaps even more so although I have yet to see if it is only with those closest to me.'

Jen's eyes shone. Peggy risked an interruption.

'Psychic abilities or empathetic energies!'

'Whatever you want to call them, I cannot now deny they exist.' Flora exchanged a glance with Jen. 'I felt something a little while ago and I didn't quite understand how much it meant - but I knew it would make someone very happy I could feel the hope emanating from this person and I knew everything was going to be all right.

'I seem to read thoughts and feelings to a certain extent, but only through empathy as you mentioned and not a conjuring trick. As I said before, I believe these feelings are there in most of us, yet seldom used to their full extent. I believe it is part of our nature and it seems that certain people of this village know how to use this gift almost unconsciously. It seems inherent in some of us. Perhaps long ago, many more people over the Earth had this gift but it has been lost to most of us.

'So that is what I believe and if that makes me, or anyone like me, a witch - or a wicce, an empath or just slightly crazy, then so be it. I'm happy to accept it as a plain fact and also as part of the birthright I have inherited.

'I do wonder if others may not have exactly the same feelings as me or any of you. Do we each have our own qualities or our own specialisms? Are we just women with highly developed senses?

Peggy answered.

'We do all seem to have our own particular field which seems to dwell within us. And yes, we feel more, understand the nature of things more, and understand nature itself more. Nature is part of who we are. The most important part.'

'I agree' Flora said enthusiastically. 'It's why my heart leapt when I saw the wildflower meadow. Not only did I feel it connected me to Sybil and - unknown to me - to all my ancestors, but also, I was glad that I could use it to help people. Like Sybil did - and like Hilde did all that time ago.

'Being how I am is why I found my mother's rowan tree without knowing it was there. It's why I suddenly know exactly how I feel after being among the trees behind this Folly. Nature has a way of telling us all we need to know.'

'You got all that from walking among trees?' Binky burst out, amazed at the rhetoric that had come from Flora.

'From the trees and I think my mum Matty had a hand in it too. I asked for her guidance.' Flora looked a little embarrassed.

'I could hear her voice in what you had to say. It's what she believed too.' Peggy said.

Jen got up and hugged Flora then remained standing.

'You two are probably aware that Steve and I have been fruitlessly trying for a baby for the last 10 years.'

'We are aware.' replied Binky. 'We join together with the power of thought to try and make it happen every year, remember?'

'To no avail because as Flora realised when she came to visit me, there was a mental block that had to be removed before I could accept I was worthy of a baby. She removed that block. So now I feel that I deserve all the happiness that a baby would bring. Which is as well. Because you also felt something else, didn't you?'

Flora smiled at her.

'Not only did she remove the block so that I could enjoy the gift of a baby. She knew that it would happen soon, as though she could feel my body change in readiness. I went to the doctor's a few days ago, I'm six weeks pregnant.'

There were exclamations of joy, then tears and a group hug. The older women knew just how Jennet had longed for a baby and had attributed much of her spikiness to the failure to conceive.

'I credit Flora with the fact that there is now a young Cayley on the way' smiled Jen with an ecstatic expression on her face.

'I think Steve might have had something to do with it too' laughed Flora as Jen blushed.

'Right' said Flora, giving Jen an extra hug, 'I have to go now, I'm helping Cal to look for this legendary Faestone again.'

Peggy muttered something to herself, watching Flora go out and then stop mid-exit.

'I've just realised. This means I will have a little niece or nephew.'

'It will be a cousin, I think' ruminated Peggy.

'I don't care. They will still be able to call me Aunt Flora' she smiled happily.

As Flora stepped onto the terrace. Peggy called after her.

'You seem to be getting on well with Calum Hythe?'

'We get on well, he seems okay' she said before marching off but Peggy had noticed the blush on her cheek.

Chapter 20

Each long-legged stride of Cal's was equal to two of her own and she was having a hard time keeping up with him. He looked back, grinned, then held his hand behind him for her to grasp. She ignored this until she tripped over a root, then grabbed the proffered hand. It felt quite nice, holding his hand, his long fingers curling round hers, him looking after her...

'Come on short–' he shouted back to her. She missed the last word, but she didn't have to guess very hard. 'If I'd known you were going to be this slow, I'd have put Fury's saddle on Finn and he could have carried you.'

'I am not short. I'm five feet ten inches which is tall for a woman.'

He laughed, knowing he'd got a rise out of her. She let go of his hand.

'I can manage, thank you. Just slacken your pace a little, we're not in a race.'

'I can't help it. I'm a moor-dweller now. I know the terrain so it's second nature.' He sighed. 'Okay, is this better?'

He slowed down to a stop so suddenly that Flora nearly crashed into him. Then she realised he was still walking but at a snail's pace.

'Oh, very funny. Go on ahead and I'll tread in your moor-dwelling footsteps' she said, trying not to smile.

Instead of concentrating on the ground. She watched Cal as he resumed his long strides. His slim body was muscly and firm. His shoulders were broad and his hair fell over his collar as he turned to check on her progress. He flashed a smile of perfect teeth. His dark eyes crinkled up with amusement as she stumbled again under his gaze. He held out his hand again and this time she kept hold.

*

'What I can't understand' said Jen is why you're making such a big fuss about it. What's wrong with Flora getting together with Cal? Doesn't she deserve a little happiness?'

'You don't understand because you weren't at the gatherings where Sybil discussed this very thing. Remember you used to be absent for quite a few of the meets?' answered Peggy.

'Well tell me now' replied Jen reasonably.

'Bianca?'

'No, you tell her you're better at remembering these things than I am.'

'Alright' said Peggy, 'You will have heard the story that Culhain tells. One of only three he relates in this village.'

'The one about Belle, the simple-minded woman who gave birth to a fairy child branded with the mark of the stag?' Jen smiled recalling the strange old man who appeared at the inn and disappeared just as suddenly when he had told his story.

'That's the one - but did you know it was a true story?'

'Well, how does anyone know it's true from all that time ago?' Jen laughed.

'Ah. There's the thing. It wasn't a long time ago. It was when you were about six years old.'

Jen sat forward

'Here? In this village? How come I've never heard anything about it?'

' Because, like Flora's 'adoption', the whole thing was hushed up. The women in question lived in a farmhouse on the moor. Belle's mother in the story was really her Aunt Ursula, as Belle's mother had died. She took the baby down to the South Coast where she brought it up as her own. The midwife was Sybil so that is how we know about it. Belle's real name was Dorcas Hythe - Cal's mother.'

*

'We're going in completely the wrong direction, away from where I saw the Faestone' Flora complained, 'It's way over that way.'

She pointed with one hand while Cal led her by the other over to a large flat boulder which had somehow deposited itself on the moors. They sat down as he produced two bars of chocolate from his pocket. She was liking this man more by the minute.

'The way I see it' he began, 'is that it isn't a fixed structure. Your great, many times, Aunt Sybil had said she'd seen it somewhere over this direction, to the left with your back to the farmhouse. When you saw it, it was over to the right from the same place.'

'Sybil told you she'd seen the Faestone? I'm surprised seeing as she didn't want to talk about the witches.'

'No, she didn't tell me personally, it was just accepted wisdom around here. Perhaps she did, perhaps she didn't. Maybe she thought talking about the witches of Farstone for my book was too intrusive, too personal? It has happened and is still happening. The stone is just a legend for most people, not personal at all.'

Flora was puzzled over this. 'But you don't think it's a legend, do you? You're quite serious about it. Can I even say obsessed?'

'You can if you want me to take that chocolate back?' he said reaching towards her, she held the remains of the chocolate away from him.

'I suppose I am a bit obsessed with finding the stone. I'm a little obsessed with this village. I first came here when I was studying for my MA in Folklore at Hertfordshire uni. It fascinated me. I felt I had found my spiritual home. It's how you told me you felt when you came here. You felt it was somewhere you belonged.'

'Yes, I remember it dawning on me gradually.'

'That's it. It was a gradual thing with me too. What really clinched it was finding out my family had owned this farmhouse before I was born. Nobody from the village remembers much about them as they kept to themselves but I found out a few things. My mother Ursula was born there. I think her parents were old Yorkshire farming stock, eking a living with sheep on the moors, selling their wool to exist.

'They weren't the type to abide by rules and were remembered for being truculent. They didn't register births or fill in censuses, so I can't discover much. The deeds to the house were lost in a fire. Fate seems to be conspiring against me. Apparently, my mother had a younger sister who died young but there's no record.' he shrugged in resignation.

'Where did you find all this out then?'

Some, like I said, from the few that remembered them, Peggy, mostly. 'My mother, when she knew she was dying, told me disjointed stories. She was on strong medication and was rambling most of the time, so I didn't take much notice. When she was coherent, she denied ever saying those things about the farmhouse on these moors but somehow, it tied in with how I felt about Farstone Moor.

'So, without any evidence about the truth of what she'd said, I came up here and it seemed like fate that the farmhouse was up for sale. It was in a terrible state but luckily I had more than enough money to put it right. It wasn't just the state of it – it was the feel of it…'

He paused and an ironic smile appeared on his face.

'Don't laugh at this – but I actually asked Sybil when I first came here to bless the house, to rid it of evil spirits' He looked embarrassed.

'And did she?'

'No, she said Peggy was the one for that. She was the one more in touch with the supernatural, and could see through the veil between the two worlds. And yes, I was that desperate. Whatever she did, it worked. It had a completely different feel when I went in after her visit. No malevolent spirits of my ancestors remained, thank god. That's why the place is completely modernised, only the outer shell remains. I'm happy enough there now though, with Fury – and that daft wolfhound.'

Finn, after galumphing ahead of them for miles, was now laid on his back with all four legs in the air.

She smiled across at him.

'I can see you are – and for what it's worth, although I didn't get any warm fluffy feelings, I didn't get any bad feelings either. The only supernatural thing I saw was you, towering over me with the lantern distorting your features. And of course, the creatures from hell that you keep in your stable and your broom cupboard.'

Cal laughed.

'That *was* fate though, the place being for sale, wasn't it?'

*

Jen look shocked.

'All that time and I had no idea that story was based on recent events. Or that Calum Hythe was the baby.'

'He's a nice boy though, isn't he?' Binky thought about how polite he'd been when he carried her groceries out to the car for her. She didn't see him in the village much. Being a writer he mostly hid himself from the world, working in isolation on his books.'

'That's what I mean' stated Jen. 'He doesn't seem like an evil fairy - though he has got the good looks of Cernunnos... without the antlers.'

'Certainly has' agreed Binky, a faraway look in her eyes.

'Will you two stop it and concentrate?' Peggy called the meeting to order.

' But' repeated Jen,' even if it's true and he is that baby–'

'Sybil said he was.' Sybil's word was law.

'Has he got the stag mark?'

'No one has been in a position to know.' replied Peggy. 'It may not be in a place that is in general view.'

At this, Binky started to drift off again with a smile on her face until Jen's voice brought her back to reality.

'Well then, he's existed on this world for what, almost twenty-nine – thirty years now, without displaying any supernatural behaviour. What makes you think he's going to start now? I mean, Belle or Dorcas or whoever, didn't seem in touch with reality, for whatever reason. I doubt very much that any of what she said is true.'

'Sybil seemed to be worried that if, when Flora came here, there would be an attraction.'

'Not hard to imagine, there aren't that many people of their ages living here.'

'She just seemed to be worried about any of their offspring having Fae blood.' Peggy replied stung by Jen's attitude.

'What the great Gardwicke heredity diluted by the blood of the despicable Fae?' said Jen, who still felt like an outsider in the Gardwicke family, as she didn't have the strong healing nature of the others.

Peggy drummed her fingers on the table, as Jen collapsed back in her chair, pressing her brow with her hands.

'I'm sorry Peggy.'

'It's fine Jennet. For what it's worth, I agree that the story about the baby Calum, may all have been a figment of a dark and troubled mind. He probably hasn't got even a drop of Fae blood' Peggy tried not to think of Culhain asking about him – or what she herself felt when she was around the lad... 'But one thing I am sure of, he has a lot of good in him and, everyone deserves a chance. So as you say, Jen, whether or not the story is true, they should be allowed to be together if they so wish.'

Peggy thought there may be something in Jen's words about Sybil being over-protective of the Gardwicke blood. It had been diluted many times but the thread of healing and empathy still ran strongly in their veins.

Again, she thought of Culhain's words when they met outside the inn. He seemed to know, just as much as Sybil, that fate had a hand in this anyway and it was best just to let it unfold. You couldn't go against fate.

'It may even be predestined' she told them and they nodded in agreement.

'I have to go to take over at the bookshop' said Jen standing up 'but I do know this. We should trust Flora. Her understanding of the mind is remarkable. She will know if there is a need to worry. She will draw back because she will feel that it's the right thing to do. She will also know if there's nothing to worry about. Her powers are strong. We must trust in her intuition and know that she will do the right thing.'

Jen kissed them both on top of their heads, the first time she had ever done so and left the Folly. 'Well, I have quite rightly been put firmly in my place by Jennet Cayley. When did she become so aware of situations as to see things this clearly?'

'Flora has been a force for good in her life' acknowledged Binky 'and perhaps after all this time she is finding her true place in the Gardwicke family. Though she wouldn't thank us for telling her that.'

*

Flora watched as Cal and Finn wrestled on the heath or rather, watched as Finn stood with an enormous paw on Cal's chest while slavering all over his face.

'Oh God Finn! It's like Niagara Falls every time you dribble. Go away and find some rabbits to play with.'

'He chases rabbits?' asked Flora thinking of Finn's gentle nature.

'No, they chase him.' Cal laughed.

As he got up the back of his tee shirt rode up, revealing what Flora thought was a tattoo.

'What's that?' she asked 'on your back.'

'Oh, it's a birthmark' he said, lifting it up again so that she could take another look. Flora did. It looked like one of those ancient cave drawings of animals. Just a few small lines that made it look like a stag with antlers

'Impressive' she said.

'The only impressive thing about me, I'm afraid.'

'Is that false modesty?' she grinned.

'Of course, I just didn't want to bore you by naming all my more impressive traits.'

He pulled her up and they started to make their way back to the farmhouse. He held her hand even though he was going at a slower pace.

It's funny, thought Flora. When she'd first come across him in demon mode, complete with lantern, she'd thought he was someone to avoid at all costs. She had started to thaw out over his gentlemanly manners on the night she had spent in his farmhouse.

She could see he had a bit of a temper but then so did she. They shared the same sense of humour. They had a lot in common and they got on well. Yet, none of this would matter too much if it hadn't been for Fury and Finn. No person who could take in and win the trust and love of abused and terrified animals like he had, could ever be bad.

From an unpromising start, where she had her doubts about him, she now felt deep within her that she could trust him. Despite his efforts to prove otherwise, she knew he was a good person.

Chapter 21

The consultation part of the business that Flora planned was taking longer than she hoped to set up. She realised early on that having the shop as a consultation room wouldn't work. Not unless she drew blinds and locked doors if she needed to examine a human patient. Otherwise, she had the problem of privacy.

So after a lot of thought she had decided to turn the little room off the shop area into a small consulting room for private matters. On enquiring as to the original use of the room, Peggy had said it was Sybil's preparation room and not a scullery. When the three-foot-wide stone shelves had come out it was surprisingly roomy, though still only big enough for a small desk, two wooden chairs and a modern but second-hand medical couch. This was in case she had to examine legs, backs, etc. to make a diagnosis.

Small animals would be given a preliminary diagnosis on-site in the shop, then she would visit these and larger animals at their own homes or farms if necessary. She couldn't take the place of a vet or a doctor. She made sure her patients knew that on the posters and the flyers she had distributed. but she could help with minor things if they trusted her. It seemed that they did trust her. People were already knocking on the side door with cats and dogs in their arms to ask for advice.

Freya came with a laconic curiosity to have a look at the animal visitors. They seemed very wary of her, which was silly as she was such a small cat and, if not quite friendly, then harmless. She hadn't grown much since that first day but appeared to be healthy.

Other people came for help to cure headaches or for a swollen elbow and other minor ailments. One woman even asked if Flora could get rid of the wrinkles on her neck. She had to tell her that that was beyond her capabilities but that the woman was attractive anyway, even with her signs of age. If she could only understand that there were more important things than looks.

There followed half an hour of tears as the woman explained how her husband had left her for a younger model. Flora gave her a pep talk, coupled with sympathy. Eventually, she sent her away with a free box of red clover tea to build her self-esteem and confidence and also a free and greatly appreciated hug.

As a result of having to paint the consulting room after the shelves came out, and all the visits, she was getting a bit behind with the online shop. It was doing very well now and she reckoned the name Wildflower Witch was helping because it had grabbed people's attention.

She had begged Philippa to let Mary help her one day a week, to put the herbs that she had prepared in sachets for the aromatic mixes, in thin cloth bags for the healing herbs and in boxes for the tea mixes. She worked in the kitchen but eventually, as she was happy to keep Mary on, she would like her to serve in the shop for one day a week. Then on another day, to carry on making up the floral and herbal products for the shop and take the rest to the post office to send out.

This was if the fearsome Philippa Reed, her mother, would let her off those two days. She was almost as scary as Peggy when she wanted to be. Flora had seen her deal with walkers who had crossed her and locals who had drunk one too many. She seemed to be fond of Flora though and was very nice to her, so fingers crossed it would be okay.

Mary herself loved working with the herbs and Philippa seemed keen for her to know a little about them. Flora wondered to herself if they were descended from one of the ancient families of the village. Maybe she thought Flora was passing down the knowledge to Mary as they had in Hilde's time, which in a way she was. She enjoyed taking Mary out into the wildflower meadow which now had another flush of different flowers pushing through to replace those that had died off or been utilised. As she learnt more from Sybil's journal about the flowers she didn't recognise, she enjoyed passing that knowledge on to Mary. It was obvious that Mary enjoyed her days at Gallipot Cottage and they usually ended the day at the patio table with a glass of wine – and Freya rubbing round their legs. Flora was glad Mary had been accepted by Freya as the little cat could be very choosy.

It was about the business that Binky Peverel knocked at Flora's door that afternoon. When the door opened, Binky only just managed to see her niece behind the big armful of wildflowers she was carrying.

'You really are Flora the Goddess of Flowers and Fertility aren't you?'

'You know my mother - Matty, told Sybil to name me Flora. It was her one wish before she died' Flora said sadly leading Binky to the kitchen table where she lay the flowers down.

'I remember' she replied 'she'd obviously had it in mind and we thought it was because of the Wildflower meadow. Which she loved and derived pleasure from as much as you do by the way.'

'It's nice to have that connection' reflected Flora, then remembered her manners. 'Would you like a cup of tea?'

'No thanks, I can't stop. I just wanted to invite you to have a stall at our fete.'

Flora knew there was a summer fete which was held yearly in the grounds of Peverel Hall. There was less than two weeks to go and Flora had doubts she could fill a stall as her stock was going out as fast as she could prepare it.

'I'd like to but I honestly don't think I can manage it as I haven't got much spare stock at the moment.'

Oh! But you must.' Binky looked stricken. She breathed out noisily. 'I know! Jennet will share a stall with you. She sells crystals and semi-precious stones, you know, which she makes into jewellery.'

'I do know' replied Flora, holding her arm towards her, showing a delicate bracelet inlaid with citrine stones. 'She made me this to bring me good luck in my business venture.'

Binky admired Jennet's handiwork before saying,

'So, does that mean you will share?'

'If Jen's happy to share then I am too. I can make extra aromatic herb sachets for aiding sleep -and concentration - and serenity and.... '

Flora's mind started whirring as she thought of the possibilities. It would be good to get her brand noticed.

'I am so pleased' beamed her aunt who then walked out of the door with a spring in her step. Flora watched her go and her eyes narrowed. There was something else something Binky wasn't telling her. Oh well, if there was she would find out soon enough. For now, she had better make another trip into the meadow so she had more supplies on the day.

*

Cal had visited later, towards the end of the day, when the flowers were at their most perfumed. They both sat on the patio chairs looking up at the still flowers, with not a breath of wind to move them. They both sat in awed silence watching the taller blooms starting to silhouette against the lowering sun, over towards the west. There was a great sense of peace as they let the sensation of nature and its power wash over them.

Eventually, he came to, as if out of a dream.

'I'm afraid I'll have to drag myself away if I want to get back before darkness descends. Luckily, I'm in the car.'

Finn looked up at him from his warm place on the patio and didn't seem in a hurry to move. Neither was Cal if he was honest with himself.

'Oh' said Fiona genuinely disappointed. 'But why did you come here in the first place?'

They had chatted easily before as usual but she knew he wasn't the type for social calls.

'Just, well, nothing really - but I might be going into splendid isolation for a few weeks so I can finish writing this book.'

' And so you can start writing The Witches of Farstone' she teased.

'Since you ask, yes' he grinned 'and I'm expecting your cooperation.'

'We shall see.'

Cal's sudden movement as he stood up made Finn jump and they both laughed before making a fuss of the big daft baby. As she saw them out she remembered Binky's visit.

'You're coming to the summer fete, aren't you?'

'Fete? Oh god, I'd forgotten about that. It's not really my thing. Besides, I might be in the last throes of Writer's Angst.'

'Do try, won't you? Binky has managed to persuade me to have a stall selling my herbal products. You've got to come and support me.'

'Binky - ah yes.' He started laughing. 'Doesn't she do her fortune-telling bit in the tent? Every year apparently.'

'Fortune-telling? That is so Binky Peverel.' She laughed too. 'I can just see her in an 'authentic' Gypsy costume, waving her hands over a crystal ball.'

Chapter 22

Binky Peverel sat in the fortune-teller's tent, practising on Flora before the fete began. She was dressed. as Flora had correctly guessed, in a full Gypsy costume complete with over-large hoop earrings. Instead of a crystal ball, there were seven tarot cards laid out on the table before her, in a horseshoe shape.

'You have had great changes in your life recently my dear' she cackled mysteriously, employing all her dubious acting skills. 'You will have gained much and found your true place in the world.'

'I wonder how on earth you know that, Madam Morgana? Your fortune-telling skills are truly uncanny' said Flora with mock amazement.

'Oh shush. I'm practising my skills on you for paying customers. Am I doing all right?'

'Sounds great. You don't tell anyone if you see anything bad do you?'

Privately, Flora was still finding it hard to believe that Binky had any skills at all in this direction. When she had mentioned this to Peggy, the older woman had told her not to be too quick to jump to conclusions.

'No, I try to steer them in the right direction away from anything bad. Okay then, I'll read your tarot properly if you want? A Celtic Cross reading I think.'

Flora wasn't sure that she *did* want - but watched as Binky laid the cards out in front of her. Binky studied the cards for a few seconds, her eyes opened wide and she put a hand to her mouth. She really was a terrible actress, thought Flora trying not to smile.

'You will have a wonderful surprise very soon. It will make your life complete' she said in a quavering voice as if it was the way fortune-tellers *should* talk.

'I'm very glad to hear that. Will it involve work money, family, romance, or my consulting room being finished off next week so I'm not waiting any longer? Now that would make my life complete.'

She watched for Binky's reaction but she wasn't taking any notice. Her eyes were fixed on the cards.

'Interesting' she said finally in a near to normal voice. 'The first thing I'm getting is that someone close to you will reveal themselves. This will be difficult to grasp but because of past events, will bring harmony into your life. Now, I see you and someone close to you will be twice-blessed with love.'

Binky suddenly frowned and Flora, as she believed now that her aunt really *was* seeing something, started to worry.

'Is it bad? Don't tell me if it's bad' she squeaked.

'No, not at all. A little confusing perhaps. There are two men who will come to mean a lot to you.'

'Two?' laughed Flora and was ignored.

'In both, the past is colliding with the present and there are issues in both their lives that need addressing before you can progress any further. Decisions that need to be made as both come to terms with the present. Do not make any of your own decisions before you feel that it is right to do so. You will know when the time comes. Let go of any resentment from past actions that will bring you pain. Your life is moving forward in the way you hoped and will bring happiness and success.'

Binky looked up at her niece with glazed eyes that gradually came into focus. She took a deep breath.

'Well!' she said in surprise then looked around her. 'Do you want me to write it down?'

'No, I'm pretty sure I'll remember it, thanks Binky. Or should I call you Aunt Bianca?'

'Nice as that is, I prefer Binky.'

' Or even Madam Morgana?' she grinned.

' At the fete' answered Binky seriously, 'yes, so I can immerse myself in my role.'

Flora grinned and went out to finish setting up the stall. Jen had arrived and had a face like thunder. She might have improved vastly but she still had a dodgy temperament.

'What's wrong?' asked Flora.

'Nothing' she scowled.

'Nothing?'

'I'm just really annoyed with…' Jen sighed and nodded over to where Madam Morgana was emerging in full splendour from the tent.

'You don't believe she can tell fortunes then?'

' What?' said Jen, confused. 'Yes, she can read the cards with great skill. It isn't that.'

Flora waited for her to continue.

'It's just that she shouldn't take matters into her own hands.'

Puzzled, Flora changed the subject.

'These crystals are beautiful. You'll have to tell me what they can do. And the gemstone jewellery, I love it' she smiled, holding up her arm with the citrine bracelet on it. Jen melted by degrees until she came around the table to give Flora a hug.

'Come on. Help me set these herbal remedies out properly so they look good next to your much prettier things.'

Jen smiled and immediately pitched in to help. There were only ten years between Flora and her aunt and though she was really pleased to have found family, she was beginning to think of Jen as a good friend as well.

*

The fete was in full swing. They had managed to get a famous but normally reclusive artist to open it. He lived in a large house on the far edge of the village on the way out. Well, the way in too as it was the only road there was, in or out. No wonder it used to get cut off in snow and still did in bad winters.

If he was reclusive, he also seemed quite friendly with it today and spent some time afterwards trying some of the stalls out. He bought an amethyst crystal from Jen and then a herb jar from Flora, to put in his studio to aid calm and creative thoughts.

Lots of these and the perfume sachets, along with her special floral teas were sold. She was so pleased as this seemed to bode well for the shop. As soon as the little consulting room was finished, she could clean the dust off the surfaces in the shop and display everything properly. She couldn't wait. The shop could possibly be open by next weekend or at least the week after. She had directed everyone on the flyers to check her website for details of the grand opening.

She had been looking after the stall as Jen had a picnic in the grounds with Steve. He had closed the bookshop for an hour and had come here to see his wife. Flora watched them laughing as they ate. Steve was as ecstatic with the baby news as Jen was. She was so happy for them both.

When Jen came back to take over, Flora walked around the fete taking it all in. She had a go at knocking the witch off her broomstick. This was Bob the butcher, dressed up complete with pointed black hat which came off every time he fell on the rubber mat - which was almost continually.

She also bought a knitted fairy in glitter wool and a crocheted witch with a black cat on her shoulder, like a feline version of Long John Silver's parrot. Flora imagined Freya viewing this with disdain. As most people knew this was the village of the Witches of Farstone, they expected things like this and looked forward to them.

Fortunately, there were many other stalls too. Tombola was run by Peggy, a raffle was run by Philippa and Mary, and Jerry, Mary's dad, ran the popular beer tent. The event was packed out as it was a gloriously sunny day. Flora made for the bakery stall, grabbing a cheese and salad breadcake for now and a scrumptious-looking cherry pie for when she got home. She asked Liv, the woman who ran the bakery, to wrap it in cling film as well as a bag, before packing them in her rucksack.

She finished her lunch in a quiet place on the grass towards the far end of the hall and away from the fete. As she put the used wrapping back in her bag, she was aware of being watched. Her skin prickled - not with fear – but with a feeling of intensity she couldn't describe.

She turned slightly towards the front of the Hall to see a tall slim fair-haired man watching her with a look of complete shock on his face. Her expression must have mirrored his when she saw his eyes - the same pale grey eyes she saw in her mirror every day - leaving no doubt in Flora's mind. This then, was her father.

Chapter 23

Flora and the man moved towards each other, step by hesitant step. Eye contact wasn't broken for a second. He looked worried, shocked, fearful and hopeful. All these impressions came to Flora as she neared him. Eventually, they stopped a few feet away from each other. He shook his head in disbelief.

'Who...? How did...?' The words were drawn out of him as though he was incapable of speech. Despite her own enormous feelings of shock over this encounter, she was shocked at something else too. For God's sake, Binky. Haven't you told him about me? Have you arranged this and left it, expecting a joyful reunion? Not even a reunion as they had never even met before. A meeting between a daughter who didn't know of this man's existence until she came here and of her father, who thought his daughter had died. Surely you've told him that I'm alive, at least?

Over his shoulder, she could see Binky and Peggy in her peripheral vision. They appeared to be arguing. When her eyes focused on Ralph Peverel again, he looked to have tears in his eyes.

'Flora is it you?' he asked in a strangled gasp. Flora's body almost collapsed in relief. At least he knew of her existence, even if he hadn't known of her presence here today.

'You know about me then?' she said in little more than a whisper.

He smiled. A gentle, friendly smile that immediately put her at ease. Just this one little gesture and she could feel the tears spring to her eyes too. No, coursing down her cheeks now. This wasn't like her yet this situation was unlike any other. Her father, her birth father stood before her, smiling at her.

'I have known about you for a while now but you had your other life and it would have been selfish of me to get in touch. You didn't know…?'

'I had no idea. Can you believe it for someone who is supposed to be sensitive to situations? I had no idea that my whole life was a lie and was about to change beyond recognition when I moved here. And I certainly didn't know I was going to meet my father.'

At this, she started sobbing but quickly drew herself back, embarrassed by her unexpected, raw show of emotion. Yet Ralph Peverel, the latest in his line, stepped forward and pulled her towards him, holding her in strong arms that comforted as a father's arms should - that felt as natural as though she had known him all her life.

'Come on Flora, let's go inside' came the softly spoken voice. 'We have a lot to catch up on'

*

Chilvers deposited the tea tray on the small table between Flora and her father. The old nanny's progress across the room had been slow and precarious, the cups shaking alarmingly in their saucers - but she made it and was rewarded with a warm smile from her former charge.

'Oh, but it's good to see you, Master Ralph. We don't see you often enough.'

Ralph squeezed her hand.

'I'm sure you'll be seeing a lot more of me in future' he said, looking over at Flora. Chilvers looked from one to the other. She had heard the tales but seeing them here together there was no doubt.

'That'll be good sir' she said with an almost toothless grin and shuffled off to the door.

Flora didn't know if she was biased but this man seemed to have wonderful qualities: kindness, understanding, empathy.'

Can I ask you…?

'You can ask me anything, my dear, and I will answer if I can.'

'My mother, Matilda'

' Matty' he said, his eyes glistening. Even now, twenty-five years later, she could have that effect on him.

'I'm supposed to look like her. Is that right? I presume it is as you recognised me straight away.'

'You are *so* like her. Your hair is even the same style and colour. Your face is the same shape. Your lips are exactly the same. The only thing is that you are taller than your mother–' Flora looked at Ralph's tall, slim frame folded up in the chair opposite.

'And…' he stared at her.

'My eyes are just like yours' she finished for him. He nodded. He suddenly plunged his hand inside his jacket and came out with his wallet. He opened it and very carefully pulled a photograph from inside. A young woman looked out at Flora.

A woman who looked just like her. She was laughing, head thrown slightly back and her eyes glinting with happiness in the reflection of the sun.

'That's wonderful. I haven't seen a photo of my mother before.'

'I will get a copy made for you' he smiled, putting it back in his wallet as though it was the most precious thing in the world.

'Yes, we were young but well, you just know if it's the right one for you don't you?' he reflected, almost to himself. She hardly dare ask but she had to.

'When you went away, I heard you were consumed by grief.'

'Oh, I was devastated. I loved Matty to distraction and I just couldn't function. I had a 'fight or flee' adrenalin reaction. I had to get away because the world was too overwhelming at that moment and I just wanted to hide. I was angry too- at everyone. I couldn't bear to think that Matty had died and that I'd never see her again. I didn't want to go on but I did then what I am still doing, threw myself into helping others so I didn't have to think about myself.'

His eyes suddenly looked worried.

'Please believe me when I say I had no idea of your existence when I left. I wasn't capable of taking anything in anyway but everyone presumed that the baby – you' he corrected himself 'had died along with Matty. Binky didn't know any different then and when she did find out chose, rightly as it turns out, not to tell me straight away.'

He looked angry for a moment and Flora realised that this wasn't an emotion that sat happily with him.

'Do you blame Sybil?' she asked quietly. He looked as if he was going to say yes until his shoulders sagged and he sat back in the chair.

'I can't honestly say that I do now, although I was angry when Binky first told me when you were about 8 years old. I was angry for quite a while and was only stopped from bringing you back to the Hall because everyone said they had no address for you, which I believed at the time.

'Looking back it was probably the right thing in the state I was in. I'd have made a rotten father at that time. Although later on when I thought about it, I would have loved to have got to know you and taken you to the places I worked abroad. There you are you see -no stability. I hate to say it but I think Sybil was right. You seem to have done well for yourself.'

He paused and looked serious.

'But what do you think? Do you think Sybil was right?'

Flora had thought about this many times but suddenly had to confront it from a different aspect. She took a deep breath.

'My parents who, I still call my parents as they brought me up, were wonderful. I appreciated them then as I appreciate them now and nothing will ever change that. From what I've heard since Sybil's revelation in her letter, I truly believe that she thought she was doing her best for me. And yes, I agree she had no choice. You couldn't have looked after me. You freely admit this. In both Sybil's and your own decision, I can see the sense in it and may have done as you each did in the same situation. Who knows?

'And I think if you had brought me up, my informative years may have been different enough to set me on a different path and I'm more than happy with the path I have followed so far. You would also have seen Matty in me and tried to bring me up in her image instead of allowing me the freedom to be myself.'

He nodded acknowledging this but she added-

'I seem to have turned out like her anyway, which says a lot for nature over nurture.'

His eyes crinkled up in amusement at this.

'Sybil couldn't have looked after me either. She'd already been left with a young child and a baby and had valiantly managed to bring them up despite having no experience of children whatsoever. When I was born, she was that much older and if she had kept me there would have been resentment both from her and Jen that they had been put in this position. Of having a reminder of what they had lost, every day.

'So yes, I do think Sybil made the right choice for you, for her, for me and for Hester and Bill Goode. It can't have been an easy choice. I know from her letters, which I will show you at some time. She did it for Jen too who needed to have time to herself without a new baby taking centre stage. You know how much she loved her older sister.'

'I do' replied Ralph 'and I'm so glad that you are good friends now.'

'So am I. I think that things in the past shouldn't cause resentment. That way lies madness. It's best to let go and enjoy what we have right now.' She gave him a special look while vaguely registering that Binky had used almost the exact words earlier. 'So, Binky has been keeping you abreast of recent events then? I have to tell you, I'm not best pleased with her at the moment.' she frowned.

Unexpectedly. Ralph laughed.

'As you get to know Binky more, you will realise there isn't a bad bone in her body. She's annoying, frustrating, airy-fairy, occasionally stupid and always completely daffy - yet she wouldn't knowingly do anything to hurt anyone.'

He looked distracted.

'She possibly saw before she asked me over here, that this meeting would be successful. When I say 'saw', I mean…'

'She saw it in the cards. Yes, she did but only after she got you over here and engineered this meeting! I think she saw something in the cards today though, which I believe. After she'd hammed it up a bit beforehand with an acting performance par excellence.'

'Ha! Typical Binky. She's an innocent, completely blameless. She got me over here with the best intentions. Ostensibly to open the fete as 'she couldn't get anyone else at short notice'. Imagine my surprise when I got over here to find myself redundant and the artist chap in my place!'

They both laughed. His eyes held Flora's.

'And I have to say that it has worked out well. I hope you agree?'

He looked worried as he waited for her answer.

'It has worked out better than I ever thought possible. I feel like I've known you forever.'

Ralph put his hands up to his face. A few seconds later, he leaned forward towards her.

'You can't believe how happy that has made me' he whispered.

What a shame this gentle and unassuming man and her lovely kind-hearted mother could not have been together throughout their lives and could not have raised her. Yet she carried within her, her mother's values and her love - and she had many years now to get to know her father.

Chapter 24

Before Flora and Ralph parted that day, They arranged for him to come round to Gallipot Cottage. She had learned he was only here until the end of the week and had to fly back early on Sunday morning from Manchester. He had tried to get someone in Nigeria to stand in for him for another week but it proved impossible.

So here she was, covered in white paint, sitting at Sybil's desk and sending 'Grand Opening' announcements on her website and other regional sites. She had spent yesterday in Beck Isle getting more posters printed to display all around there and in Farstone. Even though the consulting room would still smell of paint, she could just shut the door for Saturday. She was determined that her father would be there for her big day. Like a six-year-old with the non-speaking part of a lamb in the school nativity, she just wanted him to see how well she was doing.

Mary was at that moment stocking up the shop, according to Flora's instructions. She needed to go to Jen's soon before Ralph got here, to collect some bistro-style tables and chairs which were stored in an outhouse. The same type as the ones in the coffee area of the bookshop as it was a job lot they had bought cheaply. Flora was hoping for a good day so she could put them on the patio to let people admire the wildflower meadow and have refreshments.

There! She shut the laptop with a thankful finality. She had so much to do, she felt like she should keep moving. Making Mary a cup of coffee, she took it through, meeting her in the hallway with a cardboard box in her hands.

'Tinctures, it says' said Mary with a puzzled frown.

'Liquid herbal medicine. It's in small glass bottles so best put them on the shelf behind the counter so they don't get knocked off.'

' Right you are.' she moved off.

'Cup of coffee here for you.'

'Lovely' drifted back to Flora as she ran a brush through her hair, a contribution to tidying herself up - which didn't work - before going across to the bookshop.

'Flora!' Jen greeted her with a hug.

What a difference to their first meeting here.

'Steve's just outside getting any cobwebs with resident spiders from the tables. He'll clean them and bring them through when he's finished and carry them over for you. What on earth have you been doing? You look like Freya! Black hair with the white streak' she laughed.

'I'm a mess and Ralph's coming soon.'

She called him dad to his face and thought of him as such but it felt better calling him by name in public. She couldn't tell why but it just went along with it anyway. Perhaps a loyalty to Bill Goode? At that moment the shop door opened again.

'Ralph's already here' smiled Jen. 'I've just made a pot of coffee. Sit yourselves down at the window tables and I'll bring it across.'

She acknowledged Ralph with a cheery wave and disappeared through the door behind the counter. She'd always felt a lot in common with Ralph in their shared grief for Matty.

'I saw you coming here as I was walking up. I'm a bit early I know' he apologised.

'I'm glad you saw me. I'd have hated to miss you. We'd better do as Jen says. Steve's cleaning the tables and chairs and I'm setting them up in view of the wildflowers.'

' Ah perfect! I can help you carry them across.'

They sat down at a table which had a good view down the street towards Peverel Hall.

'I'm just about on schedule' said Flora eagerly 'I just hope I'm in time to let people know about the Big Shop Opening. At least I think the Farstone villagers will come. If only I could have advertised at the fete.'

Ralph looked guilty.

'There's no rush you know, Flora. I am proud of what you've achieved. You can show me how the famous meadow is coming along today and I don't need to be at the grand opening to know you'll make a success of it.'

Again, Binky's 'Madame Morgana' words came back to her – 'Your life is moving forward in the way you hoped and will bring happiness and success.'

' I know you don't *have* to be there but I *want* you there. I'd like to look at photos twenty years from now of an important time in my life and know that we were together on that day.'

He took her hand and squeezed it. In his mind, he was going to compare her to Matty, before he realised that although she had elements of both of them, she was her own person and shouldn't be compared to anyone.

'I will be happy to be there' he said simply. 'Have you seen the weather forecast?'

' I only use it as a very rough guide. The weather signs can be found in many natural ways without having to rely on the increasingly inexact science of meteorology.'

'So you *have* seen that it's given rain?' he said knowingly with a wink.

'Yes' she confessed 'but I have a good feeling about it, so I'm ignoring it.'

Jen arrived with two cups and a pot of strong roast coffee.

'Aren't you joining us?' asked Ralph.

'No, I'll let you two talk. I'll see you on Saturday anyway.'

Chapter 25

Ralph poured the coffee and they sat back in silence for a minute or two, enjoying the rich taste of the coffee, then Flora's brow furrowed and she took a quick sidelong glance at Ralph. Which he noticed.

'Go on' he said in resignation. 'What do you want to know?'

'I suppose I wanted to ask you... Well, we haven't talked about the 'witch thing' yet. What are your thoughts about it? Do you agree with it?'

'The 'witch thing?'' he smiled. ' If you mean do I believe in, understand and champion past present and future witches, especially our homegrown ones, then I can assure you I do. How can I not? My whole family including my direct ancestors, Matty - and now yourself, practised their craft and had a strong belief in the power of healing, faith, divination and many other forms of witchcraft. There were also the men in my family -and that means me too - who found they had a talent for healing and empathy. I have put it to good use in my work abroad. I think that's why you have that skill so strongly in yourself, as it's something that your mother and I shared.'

'I'm so glad you feel like that' said Flora 'and I didn't realise you had the skills too. I'm so happy that I came here, for many reasons of course, but it has proved to me that I am doing exactly the right thing with my life' said Flora emphatically, then pulled a wry face. 'Actually, I was a bit worried you were going to denounce all witches and say something about evil crones, poisoned apples and the devil.'

'There are no evil witches. They do a lot of good in the world. There are evil people who will be evil whatever label you put on them – including witch, but that isn't what witches do.'

'You seem more expert on them than Peggy or even Sybil' Flora said in surprise.

'You must let me show you the library up at the Hall the next time I'm over, which won't be too long now' he assured her, 'it has a wicce section of its own, from Hilde and before. I have all the written accounts of the history of Farstone and Farstone Moor since the Hall was just a large farmhouse.'

Flora remembered something else she needed to ask.

'Farstone Moor you said? What about the Fae then? Do you believe they exist?'

Ralph's eyes flickered to glance at a young man he had seen striding down the road from the entrance opposite the inn. He quickly pulled his gaze back so that Flora didn't notice.

'I believe they did exist in these parts. I believe they exist somewhere now but not always in this realm. There are still places they can trust but they are few and far between now – yet I believe they visit' he said, leaving it at that.

'If I'm honest, I'm struggling with the belief in their existence' said Flora. Her father replied unhurriedly.

'I have lived and worked in parts of Africa for many years. They have believed in their own form of witches, fairies, spirits and demons since time began and they still believe in them. What the modern world, especially the western world, has done is not prove that these things don't exist but has taken away the gift of free thinking from ordinary people. Statistics provide proof of this, that and the other not being possible, not existing. Many of us believe this without question. We believe that yes, these were all old stories from ignorant people - but were they?

'I remember our class being taught about the Christian religion, how it took over a good portion of the world and how it replaced the old pagan beliefs. Then, we were taught in schools to laugh at prehistoric man worshipping natural things like the sun, water, stars, stone trees and earth. Did we question that? Did we ever think that perhaps prehistoric man had the right ideas because they worshipped things that kept them warm, kept them alive, gave them shelter and light?

'That was the world the Fae were happiest in. A natural world. Not one that was so densely populated that there was nowhere within nature for them to exist safely any more. They didn't want to stay in a world that condemned them to storybooks as creatures who were either not real or as malevolent beings who snatched babies and unwary travellers.

'Again. I'm sure that there were bad Fae, as there are bad humans but they would be in the minority. Give this some thought...' he said to an entranced Flora. 'Just as other races have done since time immemorial, the Fae would occasionally have interbred with our own race. Not a regular occurrence as they were a proud race, keeping themselves to themselves. Yet, there may still be people walking around today with Fae blood in them, however diluted.'

He looked up again as he saw the same young man was now walking past the window, towards the shop door.

This time Flora noticed his glance and saw Cal open the door. He stood there, looking brooding, edgy, … gorgeous. Her heart skipped a beat. However lovely he was in reality, his looks still pegged him as a Byronic hero.

'Cal' she cried.

'Mary said you were here. I came to see if– but it doesn't matter' His eyes strayed to Ralph who was sitting back, studying him.

'What doesn't matter? Tell me?''

'I can see you're with Sir Ralph so I'll leave it for now.'

Flora sat there scowling. Ralph noticed this and tried to keep the smile off his face. Cal noticed the scowl too.

'Okay, okay. I know you hate not being told things. I wondered if I could borrow you for a couple of hours sometime. There's one or two things I want your opinion on up at the farmhouse.'

Flora was ready to say, of course, before she realised she was up to her eyes in work.

'I can't come up until after the weekend' she started to explain, 'It's the shop opening on Saturday and Ralph's coming around in ten minutes to have a look at how the cottage and meadow looks now'

'Of course. Yes. No problem. I understand. I should have thought before…' said Cal with politeness overkill.

'Perhaps' said Ralph speaking for the first time since Cal entered the shop, 'you could find an hour or two to go up in the morning. You probably need a break.'

Cal and Flora both looked surprised but Flora replied straight away.

'You're right, it would do me good to get away from the shop for a while.'

'That's great' smiled Cal. 'Shall I pick you up in the four-track about 9:30 tomorrow then?'

'Yes, that would work out fine.'

Just then, Steve came through carrying a newly cleaned table smelling of floral disinfectant.

'Ah, can I give you a hand with those?' Ralph asked and Jen pointed him through to a door at the back of the shop.

'They're through there' she said.

'Come on Cal, we've got to take them into Flora's garden.'

He disappeared through the door with a nervous-looking Cal following him, leaving a surprised Flora to exchange a bemused glance with Jen.

Chapter 26

Fury was behaving brilliantly. With Cal on his back he knew he could gallop away at speed, main flying in the wind, to his heart's content. Now with the lighter and more inexperienced Flora on his back, he was reining back, so to speak, and reducing his pace to a brisk trot. Flora was quite glad about this because a 16.2 hands stallion of pure muscle was a daunting sight. Even when you weren't trying to forget how high off the ground you were.

'You're doing great.' came Cal's voice from halfway up the paddock.

'I think he's being kind. He feels sorry for me' shouted Flora while concentrating hard.

'Rubbish. He likes you and you know it. I think the feeling's mutual.'

'Of course it is, he's magnificent' she said, patting Fury's neck as she brought him to a halt in front of Cal.

'Do you feel confident enough now? Just in case you have to ride him when I'm not here?'

'I do. Although I might need another lesson in saddling up before you hightail it to London.'

Cal had asked Flora to look after the animals on the occasions that Dylan, the vet's assistant, couldn't make it. That was one of the things Cal had wanted to ask her, but he needed to know that she was comfortable with the animals first. He knew Finn would love her to be there, but Fury was a little harder to handle. However, he was as gentle as a lamb with her today.

His latest book, Folk Tales of the Wild Moors was due out in a week's time and he was going to have to spend more time away than usual with launches, signings and interviews. Flora hadn't realised he was the second most prominent UK expert in his field, the first being the university professor who taught him - and he was quite famous with it.

She took Fury back to the stable, took his saddle and bridle off and rubbed him down. Then they took one of the blankets, laying it on the grass outside the gate and took in the view.

There was a heat haze over the newly-blooming heather. Cal looked up at the sky.

'Storm coming, do you think?'

Flora's shoulders collapsed.

'Oh, don't say that! I want it to be sunny and perfect on Saturday.'

He laughed.

'But you know what it's like around here from personal experience.'

' I remember it well and it's not something I'd like to repeat.'

'You know, when I thought about it afterwards, you could have died. You had no idea where you were and you could have wandered the moors all night, disorientated, freezing cold and drenched to the skin. It would have been a toss-up then between hypothermia or pneumonia that finished you off - or both. You wouldn't have survived.'

'Peggy told me that too and I thought the same.'

'I also thought that perhaps the Faestone appeared to you because you were in desperate need and it appeared to you at that particular place' he nodded in the direction she had seen it, 'because they knew the farmhouse was nearby.'

'They being...'

'The Fae. Which in turn leads me to believe that they have had a bad press. They wanted to save you and sent you down to me.'

'Look I'm only just coming to terms with the possibility of the Fae's existence, mostly due to you and Ralph. So don't overwhelm me with things like fairy do-gooders. Whoever or whatever guided me toward you. I'm very grateful' she said, for more than one reason, she added to herself.

Cal had gone quiet and was staring into the distance.

' Cal. Are you okay?'

' What? Oh yes, I was just thinking.'

Flora waited.

'Half the winters I've spent up here have been pretty bad. I've been cut off many times. It doesn't usually bother me but...'

'It does now? Why?'

Cal looked uncomfortable.

'Sometimes I think it would just be nice to be in the village '

He looked furtively up at Flora and saw she was staring at him. He felt the colour rise to his cheeks as he continued quickly.

'Well, it would just be nice to be able to walk to the shops in bad weather. Have a drink at the inn.'

'But I thought you loved the farmhouse? Your ancestral home?'

'Mmm' he murmured

'You don't?' she said incredulously.

'I do - of course I do. But it's quite often inconvenient and I've come to realise why it was abandoned in the first place. The cost of keeping the propane generator going alone is astronomical. I mostly live with oil lanterns and log fires. And I have to write everything by hand as there's no Wi-Fi out here. I can use a satellite phone at least, which is what I told Frank.

'Frank?'

'Yes, he's the Moors Rescue team leader. When they're up on exercise around here, they sometimes call for a cup of tea. He's often said if I wanted to sell the place, he'd buy it and he would live here - he's a real outdoor sort of person - and the others could use it as a base. One person staying there with him on a rota throughout the week, so there were always at least two people to cover any emergency until the others got there.'

Flora shook her head.

'I can't believe you're even thinking about selling it' she said.

'I think selling it might be a step too far to be honest, although there is a possibility of renting it to them.'

Privately she thought it might be a good idea but for selfish reasons she didn't want to think too hard about, but he had spent time and effort on it. It was his family home, for heaven's sake.

'That was the other thing I wanted to ask you about but the question is academic anyway.'

'How so?' she asked.

He looked at Finn lolling on the ground in front of them.

'Fury' he said simply. 'I think Finn would be fine now. He seems to be more used to people and would fit in with village life better but Fury?'

He shook his head. 'How many houses in the village have stables?'

'Oh God! Yes.' Flora thought for a moment. 'You wouldn't want to move further afield then? To somewhere more suited to Fury?'

Cal drew back like he'd been hit in the face. He recovered quickly.

'No, I may have become more aware of the impracticalities of a remote farmhouse on

Farstone Moor, but I still love the village. I still feel at home here and both Fury and Finn would miss their exercise on this moor, it's perfect for them.'

He got up and Flora followed suit, watching him closely. He pulled the blanket up and started folding it distractedly, hanging it over the gate. He turned to look at her, his features unsettled.

'Do *you* think I should move away?' he asked hesitantly. She looked into his dark troubled eyes that echoed the same emotions that she was feeling. She would as soon see him move to another place as she would see herself moving away from the village. They both belonged here. Together. Whatever Cal saw in her eyes, it was enough for him to move a step closer.

'I don't want you to move away from the village Cal.' she said quietly and sincerely.

He squeezed his eyes shut, then opening them, reached forward to gently pull her in towards his chest. She put her head against it, enjoying the sensation of his strong arms holding her. As she put her head back to look at him, his lips met hers and she gave herself up to the inevitable. Was this love? It certainly felt like it.

Her eyes shone as he moved back, still holding her face between his hands.

'I'm very glad you feel that way, Flora' he smiled, making her go weak at the knees. She recovered quickly.

'Well.' she grinned, 'if you moved, I'd miss seeing Finn and Fury wouldn't I?'

Finn jumped around them like a demented gazelle as Cal chased Flora round in circles, both of them laughing happily.

Chapter 27

The Grand Opening

People were starting to drift into the garden of Gallipot Cottage. Outside the shop, there was a 'Welcome to the Wildflower Witch' handwritten notice and a big red arrow directing them into the shop.

At the side of the cottage, next to the open gate in the hedge, there was another sign. 'Open day - Welcome to the Wildflower Meadow'. Yet another red arrow pointed them through, towards the patio. It was on this patio that Flora was running backwards and forwards with a certain degree of panic which was most unlike her. She just wanted everything to be perfect.

Freya sat on a low wall at the side watching Flora with the knowing eyes of one who was experienced at chasing their own tail. There was a certain patronising look too. Cats were like that. Though she seemed perfectly happy with proceedings and blinked at Flora as she dashed by, no doubt conveying subliminal messages of 'What's the hurry? Take your time. Enjoy it. Prrr.'

On a table at the back of the cottage next to the back door, were leaflets printed by Ralph, detailing the history of the wildflower meadow. Of its origins with Hilde and of the story of the Wildflower Witch name that started with Sybil. Flora and Ralph had written them together.

Inside the shop, people were starting to congregate. It was only twenty minutes since it had opened and already it was full. Mary was serving but had been joined by Peggy. Not known for being a 'people person', Flora had expected Peggy to refuse when she'd asked her to help in the shop. Peggy had surprised her by saying she would because she was so pleased that Sybil's legacy, along with those before her, was being carried on.

Mary's innocent enthusiasm in serving the customers was being tempered by Peggy's usual pragmatism, she was merely getting on with the job. She wrapped the products in pretty eco bags and took the money. She even smiled occasionally...

In the kitchen. Liv was placing her scones, cream cakes and fruitcake on plates as the orders came in. It was only 9:45 a.m. They had only expected to be serving hot drinks at this time. But people seemed to want the full experience.

The sun shone down on them. Flora's 'good feeling' had manifested itself into a perfect day. Brilliant blue skies without a cloud to be seen and a warmth which didn't burn but caressed. The rain, which had fallen all the previous day, had painted all the wildflowers in even more vivid colours than normal and the grass in a brighter green. The effect as you sat drinking your coffee and eating your scones, was wonderful. The colours shone jewel-like shining in the sun's rays and providing a living visual experience which transcended any artist's painting.

The day went on with more and more people filling the shop and the patio. How had so many people got to know about it in such a short space of time, thought Flora? It exceeded her expectations by a great deal. Everyone was positive, sincere compliments were given and the stock in the shop went down so drastically that

Flora saw herself wandering the meadow for eternity, gathering more supplies.

Many people said that they would be coming to her for the natural remedies *and* for the natural healing advice she advertised too. They were shown the consulting room by an eager Binky who extolled the virtues of Nature's healing. Her stellar performance had many people hanging on her every word. Flora wasn't sure half the tales she told were true but the idea behind them was - Nature had everything you needed. Whatever minor ailment you had - there was a cure in Nature.

She was glad to hear Binky tell everyone that of course, more serious problems couldn't be cured this way, but a good herbalist, like the Wildflower Witch was, would tell you this and point you in the direction of the doctor's surgery.

Meanwhile, outside in the wildflower meadow, Flora was kept busy explaining the names and uses of the flowers there to the people who wandered up and down the beautiful, colourful oasis. She loved how genuinely interested they were and loved even more that, in general, natural products seemed to be gaining popularity. She wasn't just happy for the sake of the business but for the sake of the world as a whole.

Flora, Ralph and Binky when she wasn't giving her performances, waited on the many customers from morning until they closed. When the customers heard Sir Ralph Peverel from Peverel Hall was serving them, they were tickled pink. The custom in both the shop and the makeshift cafe on Flora's patio was non-stop all day with no respite.

It was with considerable relief that Flora finally locked the shop door - nearer to 6:00 p.m. than the advertised 5:00 p.m. - took both the signs down and collapsed in one of Jen's borrowed chairs. Jen, who had kept the bookshop open all day on Flora's advice in case of opportunist sales, collapsed opposite her.

'We've had our best day in months, you were right in telling us to keep it open' she said 'I still feel guilty though in not helping you out.'

'You helped us over lunchtime, the busiest period. It's been a fantastic day, hasn't it?'

'Flora, I can't believe what you've brought to this village. You've brought a vitality that has energised the whole place. Never mind the joy you've brought to me personally.'

They exchanged happy smiles.

'My back!' complained Peggy, 'if I'd have known I was going to be on my feet all day...'

'I brought you a stool to sit on behind the counter' protested Mary.

'Didn't have time for sitting' Peggy said, starting to smile.

'It's alright Mary, she's not happy unless she's complaining' laughed Jen.

'You enjoyed yourself then, Peggy?' Flora asked.

'If you call a bad back, aching limbs and people-overload enjoying yourself then, I suppose it wasn't too bad' she admitted grudgingly as Jen and Flora exchanged grins.

'Glad to hear that because I was thinking of asking you to help out preparing the herbal products so that Mary can serve in the shop. That's second nature to you, isn't it? Reasonable rate of pay considering you get lunch and copious amounts of tea and coffee.'

Flora wasn't sure which way this was going to go.

'Really?' asked Peggy slowly.

'Yes, only one or maybe two days a week, whatever suits you. What do you think?'

Jen held her breath. She knew Peggy of old.

'I reckon I could manage that.' Peggy looked as though she couldn't care less but Flora could tell she was secretly pleased. 'And what will you be doing while Mary and I are holding the fort?' Peggy continued with a wink.

'Don't you worry' laughed Flora, 'I've got plenty to keep me occupied with my online business and preparing the products for that, as well as serving in the shop a couple of days a week.'

Binky came out onto the patio.

'Shall we break open the champagne?'

Ralph and Binky had provided half a dozen bottles from their cellar in anticipation of the celebration afterwards.

'I'd say that's a very good idea' said Flora, calling Liv through from the kitchen. Philippa had been helping Liv out in the morning, but like Jen, had gone on to enjoy a bumper day at the Peverel Arms, due entirely to the presence of Flora's customers.

Flora brought another two bottles through from the kitchen and looked around for Ralph's help to open them. She saw he was over in the far corner talking to Cal who had turned up a couple of hours ago. He had Finn with him who, although slightly overwhelmed by the sheer volume of people around him, had taken it all in his stride. He kept firmly by Cal's side though. Rome wasn't built in a day.

She knew Cal would have to go back to his farmhouse before nightfall to settle Fury down. She accepted this but it would have been nice if he could stay... No- it was no good her wishing. She understood. Fury and Finn came first.

Chapter 28

Ralph Peverel leant against the stone wall bordering the wildflower meadow. He was in earnest conversation with Cal, the young man, whom his daughter had chosen to spend a lot of her time with. The man in question leant against the same wall and looked up at the myriad of colours, reaching up to Pookey Wood. It was a magical place and he knew without having to be told, that there was no reason why Flora had to move away from this and onto the bleak moor, just to be with him. He understood.

'So Flora tells me you may be wanting to sell your place and move to the village?' said Ralph not only cutting into Cal's silence but also echoing the thoughts moving around his head right now. He looked up, surprised.

'She didn't think she was betraying a confidence' Ralph said with a frown.

'No, no she wasn't. I suppose she told you why I would like to sell up – or rent somewhere else - and also the reasons why I can't.'

He felt unaccountably nervous around Ralph and not just because he was Flora's natural father. There was something else that he couldn't quite put his finger on. Yet Ralph exuded goodwill which Cal felt was completely genuine. He watched as the older man processed his thoughts.

'I have a suggestion.' Ralph said eventually. I haven't had too much time to think about it as yet or what it would mean. So bear with me as I process my thoughts out loud.'

Cal frowned, wondering what on earth was coming next.

'There is a property on my estate' continued Ralph. 'Gardeners Cottage, so-called for obvious reasons. Although having said that, it was what once housed the grooms for the stables that were next door. You probably won't have seen it.'

Cal thought back to his infrequent visits to the grounds in six years. He knew of the Folly, although he hadn't seen it - but hadn't seen any other buildings in the grounds. He shook his head.

'Gardeners Cottage had been used in more recent years to house the groundsman and his wife. When they died and the Peterson family from the village took over the job, the small barn between the house and the stables was converted just after the war to add more living space to the cottage, for my aunt and her family to live in. The property is now empty as one cousin is in America and the other in Australia, both permanently. You probably knew that the Petersons who look after the grounds now, have their own house in the village, which their family have lived in for generations?'

Cal nodded even though he had only vaguely heard of the Peterson family and then only because he knew that they were one of the original old families of Farstone.

'I don't like houses lying empty' declared Ralph. 'It is damaging to them if they're not lived in. I don't want to sell it and break the estate up. You can understand that?' he looked at Cal for confirmation and he nodded, 'but I would be willing to rent it out to you. The stables are attached to the cottage so Fury would be close by. There are vast amounts of grounds around it where Finn could run around undisturbed. It is backed by a spinney and surrounded by acres of land.'

Cal stood open-mouthed.

'I'm sure we could come to a reasonable agreement regarding rent and conditions. Basically, I would just want you to look after it so it doesn't fall into disrepair. The stables too.'

'I don't know what to say' Cal gulped.

' "I'll think about it" would be a start' smiled Ralph. 'I also think it might be a nice place for you to write your books. There will be good Wi-Fi reception apparently, as there is at the Hall. While not isolated, it is in a very private place and can't be seen from the Hall or the village. You won't be disturbed.'

'Wow,' Cal breathed out. 'It's definitely enticing. Have you talked to Flora about it?'

'No, I thought I'd talk to you first. I didn't want to disappoint her if you refused.'

'You think it would disappoint her? Cal asked a little too eagerly.

Ralph laughed. 'I think she might be but she is her own person. Who knows what she may think?'

There was a note of pride in his voice. Was it really only a week that he'd known her? It felt like much longer.

'I also have an ulterior motive. Eventually, not for a while yet hopefully, Flora will inherit Peverel Hall. I don't think it has entered her head yet that she is my only heir.'

'There's time yet, surely?' frowned Cal. Ralph couldn't have been much older than fifty, if that.

'No, I don't think so. I can say 99.5% definitely not, allowing for chance - but Flora would be the eldest anyway. I believe the firstborn should inherit, whatever gender they are. It would be nice to know that you're nearby for now, perhaps with Flora visiting you and getting to know the place before she does have to take over, many years hence.'

It felt to Cal like he was in a dream where his whole life was predestined. He should feel annoyed, manipulated, used. He was a very proud person. Yet he couldn't see any downsides to it. In many ways, it was exactly what he wanted. He would have Fury nearby in the stables and if he was cut off from the world in winter he would at least be cut off along with the rest of the community, with the shops close at hand. He would be near to Flora...

'Have you thought of the difficulty in getting Flora to move to the Hall in the future?' Cal asked. 'I'm not sure she'll ever leave Gallipot Cottage.' They both automatically looked over at Flora who was animatedly talking to Peggy and holding a bottle of champagne in her hand.

'No, you're right. I think she has a connection to this place that will never be broken. However, I'm hoping not to shuffle off this mortal coil for a good few years yet. Binky too, I hope, is going to be around for a good many years. So when the time does come. it's likely that Flora will have children of her own, grown up by that time perhaps, who can take over Gallipot Cottage and the business. Or even Jen's offspring could - or even Mary...'

'Hasn't it got to be a Gardwicke?'

Ralph nodded.

'Or have Gardwicke blood, according to the legend' was all he would say.

Cal's brows knitted together, pondering on the logistics. He knew he wanted Flora to be in his life from now on but would they be able to live together? Could they have separate houses but still have a good, loving relationship?

He was going to have to talk to Flora. He had been putting it off. She would know what to do, he felt sure. His brow lifted and the worry in his eyes cleared. Flora would know.

Ralph watched him in silence before a shout interrupted both their thoughts.

'Come on you two! You'll miss the fun bit' grinned Flora, holding up the champagne and a glass.

Chapter 29

The evening had a lazy, languorous quality to it. The light didn't seem to be real, it was soft and indistinct. The sky was the strange muted colour that came when the day had been as sunny and hot as today and it didn't want to give in to the night.

Everyone was still sitting on the chairs outside, some with their faces up to the retreating sun, catching the last of its rays before they lost their strength. For the last five minutes, no one had spoken. They had been talking non-stop as the champagne flowed earlier - but now it was as if the evening had cast its magic spell over them. A glass was lifted occasionally but in general, there was no movement.

Only the taller stalks of the wildflowers caught the breath of the breeze and moved ethereally as if caught in the same spell. The blooms were being caressed by the glimmer of the evening sun as it played down on them and the trees next to the stone boundary wall showed a golden glow, displaying it proudly to all the garden's residents.

Flora could see Pookey wood beyond the meadow. It was mostly now in silhouette but with the very tops catching the sun. She could see the rowan tree planted for her mother and her thoughts went back to an hour ago when she had taken her father up to see it. He had been offered the chance years ago but wouldn't take it. He thought it might have been where she had died until Flora explained it was just her ashes and a memorial tree. Then he allowed her to show him.

*

'Just wait there a moment.'

He smiled at her as they walked slowly up the narrow, central grass path between the flowers, watching the bees flit between the blooms. He reached for a multi-purpose pen knife in an inner pocket. She laughed.

'I bet you were a boy scout.'

'I was - but you wouldn't believe how handy these have been in my work. And now, with your permission?'

'Of course' she smiled.

He moved amongst the wildflowers, picking the brightest and most beautiful, as Matty had been to him. Then he followed their daughter up to the wood. He knew even before Flora told him, that this was the tree. The rowan for protection watching over what would have been her cottage. She would be so pleased it had passed to her daughter. Flora….they had discussed the name. She had been sure it was a girl and of course, she had been right.

He walked forward. He could see that there was twine wrapped loosely around the tree and suspected that Flora had been doing exactly the same as him. He reached out and put the bunch of flowers inside the twine. A fitting tribute from some*where* she had loved and from some*one* she loved.

'I'll leave you alone for a while' said Flora.

'Perhaps later but for now I think she would like to feel we are together, saying hello to her.'

Flora went up to him and he put his arm around her. They both faced the tree. Ralph began to speak in a low, rhythmic voice.

'Matty. I know you are there and listening to us. We both love you so much. I will never forget you and I will make sure our daughter knows all about you. I believe you have engineered this somehow' he smiled.

'You could always wind us round your little finger – Sybil, Binky - and especially me. Believe me, finding our daughter after all these years is the best thing that's ever happened to me since I met you. I promise you now that I will stop wandering the earth trying to forget but will at long last stay here and remember. We love you, Matty. Brightest blessings, my darling'

He squeezed Flora's shoulder so hard it hurt. They were both in tears with Flora sobbing quietly. After a minute or two to gather themselves, they turned to go back down to the others. Flora put a hand on his arm.

'You said you would stay here. Did you mean it?'

'Flora, I have neglected my duties for far too long and left Binky dropped in at the deep end. I am not neglecting you now. I have decided to come back to be near you, my sister and my home. What I will do I am less sure of. I do know that I will set things in motion when I return to Africa tomorrow.'

Flora hugged him and they both went down the path laughing and trying to avoid tripping over the little black cat.

*

Now on the patio, Liv, Jen - and Steve who had come to join his wife - were starting to make a move. Jen started to clear up the coffee cups and champagne glasses they had used, to take into the kitchen.

'Leave those Jen. I'll do it later' said Flora, 'My brain is buzzing so much, I don't think I'll sleep at all tonight.'

'I'm not surprised. What a successful day you've had. One we've all shared, thanks to you. The best thing about it is that you're not coming here with modern, opposing ideas that disrupt the balance of the village. Although you've injected new life into it, you are also bringing age-old traditions, almost back from the dead. Generations of Gardwickes will be thanking you!'

Jen laughed but Flora knew that, however sarcastic she wanted to sound, she was at last starting to feel like she was part of the Gardwicke family and part of Farstone itself.

They all hugged and as Flora let go of Jen, she patted her stomach and started to say

'and don't forget young–' She stopped suddenly.

'No, don't tell me if it's a girl or a boy. I don't want to know' laughed Jen.

'I honestly can't tell at the moment it could be either. Mixed messages?'

She shrugged as she tried to explain but Jen was already on her way out. Strange, thought Flora, it was as if... She looked across at Binky who probably had no recollection of her prophecy, but it came back to Flora like it had slapped her in the face. She smiled to herself. That's it, she thought.

Passing the others on the way out of the gate was a young, healthy-looking man with blond curls and red cheeks. There was a shriek from Mary which she tried unsuccessfully to subdue. She ran over to him. Flora looked from one to the other and noticed their embarrassed smiles.

I er - I wondered if Mary wanted someone to walk her home?' the lad stammered.

...And you just happened to be passing... Flora tried to stop her thoughts putting a smile on her face.

'Yes please' said Mary, going over to his side and gazing up into his face. 'Oh, Flora, this is Arnie Peterson.'

'Pleased to meet you' she smiled after waiting a few seconds in vain for the addition of 'my boyfriend'. It was probably a very new romance.

They went out into the street, arm in arm and she went back to sit down. Cal and her father had deserted her. They seemed to be getting very pally over there at the far table, heads together in discussion again.

The sun had started to set, giving the whole garden, meadow and wood that mystical quality that made you believe that anything was possible. That mythical creatures may come out of the woods and off the moors. It was the sort of evening that made you happy to be alive. Binky broke into Flora's spiritual thoughts with a distinctly unspiritual utterance.

'Peggy! Stop snoring. You sound like an old warthog with its head underwater. Come on.'

She prodded Peggy who then sat up and said promptly,

' I wasn't asleep. I was just resting my eyes' to general derision and loud laughter.

'I didn't realise that shutting your eyes made such a loud noise' grinned Binky, winking at Flora. 'Come on. We'd better be going home, sun's nearly down.'

'We're not vampires dear' said Peggy, getting up to give as good as she got.

Flora hugged them both. She couldn't imagine life without them now - or any of them. She felt incredibly happy and this village was her happy place. Ralph hurried over, also hugging Flora then he put his forehead against hers.

'I have to go' he said reluctantly. 'I have a ridiculously early start tomorrow but believe me, I will be back as soon as I can.'

She believed him.

They all walked towards the gate together, leaving just Cal and Finn in the garden, which was now almost in the semi-darkness of a beautiful summer's night.

Chapter 30

As soon as they came out of Flora's, Peggy saw him. Half-hidden in shadows and standing on the opposite corner under the street signs.

She saw Binky cross the road diagonally past him seeming as if she hadn't seen him at all, which she probably hadn't. She wasn't sure about Ralph's reaction or if he would notice him as she had no experience of him recently. What she saw surprised her.

He walked across to the figure and they both stood there for uncounted moments until Ralph stepped back. He bent his head down in a gesture of respect and what puzzled Peggy even more was that the figure followed suit. Their dutiful reverences over, Ralph continued on his way with a brief look back at Peggy. The figure turned his face towards her or would have done if his face had been visible. Perhaps he would allow her to glimpse it again, but - perhaps not.

She crossed over to him, she knew her place, and stood in front of him. He spoke first, in that voice that you couldn't remember afterwards, as though it had drifted in on the air.

'Margaret Harker'

'Culhain' she greeted him. He acknowledged this with a tilt of his head.

'She has surpassed expectations.' he said. Peggy nodded. There was a silence.

'He has made good progress too' she said, to fill the silence.

'That is so.'

He was obviously invested in their well-being. Peggy now privately thought about the connection between Culhain and the boy. Was he a messenger, reporting back – or something more? At least he knew the boy was someone to be proud of.

Then she took in a horrified breath until it rattled in her throat, when she realised there were no private thoughts where Culhain appeared. After an interminable moment for Peggy, he said,

'Yes, someone to be proud of.'

She hung her head in embarrassment. She wanted to ask if everything would be okay but when she looked up to ask him, there was no one to be seen - but his voice could still be heard, close by.

' Things are as they should be.'

She felt he was still there but finished with her until the next time – yet those words were all she needed to know. She turned for her home.

*

Cal wandered over to Flora with a nonchalance that she knew he didn't feel. How someone could be so nervous, so loving, so generous and kind, whilst looking physically as though he could scowl for Britain and crush a thousand Victorian maiden's hearts, into the bargain, she just didn't know.

Finn greeted her first, nearly knocking her over in the process. She looked up at Cal and suddenly didn't want him to go. A forlorn hope.

'Have another glass of champagne' she said.

' I have to get back to Fury' he started to say apologetically 'but another? I haven't even had one yet, I'm driving.' He had left his four-track in the driveway behind Flora's car.

'Oh well then, just a very small one, because you have to celebrate my first successful day at Wildflower Witch.'

'One of many I hope' he said accepting the half-filled glass.

'It's been' Flora struggled for words and settled for the old standby... 'Wonderful!'

'It has' agreed Cal, reaching for her, pulling her towards him. He bent his head down to kiss her lips and lost himself in the love, passion and comfort he found there. Pushing themselves apart reluctantly they sat down, chairs touching so their bodies could too. They toasted each other with what was left of the champagne.

'Here's to you and the Wildflower Witch' he said.

She reached across and kissed him again.

'And here's to us?' she asked.

'And here's to us' he replied. He grabbed her spare hand with his and they gripped each other tightly.

'There might be a way around this.' Their thoughts were obviously tuned to the same wavelength as Flora immediately knew what he meant. She didn't speak but waited for him to elaborate.

'Sir Ralph... Ralph...' he looked awkward then finally decided 'your father - has come up with a suggestion. Apparently, you mentioned my little dilemma to him.'

Flora had the grace to look embarrassed.

'I just felt it was the right thing to do' she said apologetically.

'I think that's probably true. Let's see if you agree.' He proceeded to tell her of his earlier conversation with her father and was rewarded with a happy beaming smile followed by a kiss that held the promise of a glorious future.

*

As Cal went into the driveway, he opened the back door to let Finn galumph into the backseat. As he opened the driver's door, he thought he caught sight of someone across the road but when he turned towards there, the place was deserted. Instead of feeling disturbed, he felt strangely elated. He smiled to himself and backed out, then drove up to the farmhouse on the moors.

Epilogue

The Folly was decked out in style. Fairy lights hung from the ceiling and wrapped around the trees near the entrance. Chinese-style lanterns hung from branches and pointed the way from Peverel Hall along the tree-lined path, to arguably an even more important building than the Hall itself.

It had seen gatherings to urgently discuss village business – from recent times and back to the Witch Hunts. Anything of importance to do with the village since the building was built, had been discussed here. Indeed, an earlier Ralph Peverel had it built originally for that purpose.

Yet many, many years before this, the Wicce of Farstone, had gathered on this site. It was far in the depths of a large wood at that time. After giving their thanks to the Natural Deities, the wicce would discuss the issues that involved them at the time. They would also celebrate the turning of the year, the pivotal moments of the natural calendar. Today, their descendants were celebrating here again.

Jennet Cayley nee Gardwicke had given birth two weeks ago and mother, father and each baby were in attendance.

'Twins!' said Binky in delight. 'I can't believe it.'

'I don't know why' Flora laughed. 'You predicted it at the fete, Madam Morgana.'

'Me? Oh, that would have been my unconscious mind' Binky said, knowingly.

'Your mind is always unconscious' mumbled Peggy with a grin at Flora.

'"Someone close to you will be twice blessed with love," you said' repeated Flora.

She also remembered her saying that two men would come to meet a lot to her – and that her new life would bring happiness and success. Right on all counts, Binky.

'I'm sorry I kept it from you all after we had the last ultrasound, we wanted it to be a surprise but, it wasn't a surprise to you Flora, was it? After your Wildflower Witch launch party, you felt something. I know you did.'

'You're right. I couldn't tell if it was male or female because it seemed to be both. Then I realised, it *was* both.'

Emma and John peeped up at her, gurgling happily. Emma was both Matty's middle name and the name of Sybil's mother. Jen had wanted to leave the name Matilda for Flora, she'd said - 'just in case'.

'John was your father's name, Steve?'

' It was' he replied immediately with a smile, glad to see friends and family gather around his twins, giving them protection, 'but it is also a family name in Jen's family – your family too of course. So the continuation is there.'

Mary had come with Arnie and was now making a fuss of the twins. She and Arnie had recently announced their engagement and it seemed that babies were uppermost in her mind.

'Did it hurt?' she asked Jen.

'Hurt like hell' she answered.

There was a pause.

'Nah, you're teasing me' Mary laughed- an innocent in a hard world.

'I'm not really' said Jen honestly, 'but I can tell you now, it is most definitely worth it.'

They both looked at the babies, dark fluffy hair framing their chubby little faces.

'I love my niece and nephew' Flora said. 'Okay, cousins...' she amended after glancing at Peggy's raised eyebrows.

Flora could see Ralph at the far end of the table. Cal, Steve and Arnie had joined him and they were in animated conversation about the estate. Her father looked up and caught her eye, giving her the tenderest smile before returning to the business in hand.

He had been true to his word and left his job in Africa as soon as a suitable substitute could be found. He had thrown himself into village life and the well-being of the village, hence the discussion about opening an unused barn in the courtyard area of Peverel Hall as the Farstone Witchcraft and Faerie Museum.

Binky the actress was very much looking forward to acting the part of a witch. If it took a long black cloak, a tall black hat and a stuffed cat to do it, then so be it. Even though she knew this had nothing to do with real witches, she would suffer for her art.

Cal walked towards Flora. She still got that thrill when she watched him. Physically, he was perfect. He wasn't far from that otherwise, she had to admit. Finn was incongruously jumping up and down outside with the small black cat that had adopted Flora recently, since the shop opening. Not Freya. This one was pure black and she had named it Rowan. She worried that Freya would have her nose put out of joint but the young cat seemed to sense that Rowan belonged with Flora and had very happily defected to live with Peggy. There seemed to be a mutual understanding between the old woman and the haughty little cat.

Fury, meanwhile, was stabled safely, securely, warmly and happily up at Gardener's Cottage. The move had been beneficial to all three of them. They had the same freedom but in more conducive surroundings and when they wanted to 'let go', which all of them did at some point, including Cal, they only had to go across to the moors.

There was talk of Flora and him collaborating on the book but only on the *historic* Witches of Farstone. She didn't want anyone in living memory mentioned in it.

Flora spent a lot of her time up at Gardener's Cottage, days - and nights. Yet Gallipot Cottage was home. In an increasingly changing world for her, this arrangement between them didn't seem so strange after all. Perhaps in the future... well - who knows?

Peggy sat in her place at the head of the table. She raised her glass towards everyone as they raised theirs to her. She thought of how the old order had been dying out and how it had been rejuvenated with the arrival of Flora.

The little black cat with the white streak sat on the nearby chair and surveyed the proceedings with a superior eye. The old woman raised her glass to the cat, who blinked and purred.

'All is as it should be' thought Peggy, with a contented smile.

Acknowledgements

I would like to thank Debbi and Charley at **Mystic Spellpot** – 'The Little Shop for Mystical People and Magical Items' in Bridlington, East Yorkshire. They have taken the time to advise me on certain elements of Witches and Healing, which I have incorporated into this book.

Above all, they showed me that witches are normal people – neither of them wore tall pointed black hats, though I did spy a broomstick behind the counter…

Debbi also gave me a herb vial to aid concentration and inspiration, which I badly needed at that point. She told me to burn a yellow candle when I opened it – and I have to say it worked, as my writer's block disappeared.

They said a healthy respect for Nature is uppermost for a witch. Healers too, make use of Nature, as in the wildflower meadow but their intention and focus are just as much a part of the healing process. Flora uses this almost as much as her potions and remedies made from the Wildflower meadow.

Divination, whether by the tarot or other methods, is also practised by witches and, learning how to read the cards or the signs is central to this - as demonstrated by Binky, in rare serious mode, in the book.

An important aspect of the life of witches is Belief, Trust and Instinct. Witches also believe that abilities can be passed down through families – as with Sybil and Flora and countless generations before them.

Their information has helped shape this book – so, thank you, Debbi and Charley. Any mistakes are solely mine.

As well as at the shop, you can find them on Facebook.

Notes

Just a word about the differing information and beliefs to be found on the web regarding all aspects of Witchcraft. It is confusing because different people believe different things – or follow their own path (which sounds good to me.)

Many people don't agree on basic matters, including greetings. Blessed Be, for instance, is used by some but belittled by others. So I have just gone off at a tangent sometimes and have used whichever I want. At other times and with other matters, I have just used my imagination, which after all is what writers do.

I haven't mentioned the Fae who play an important part here… but I'm sure I can leave you to make your own mind up on *their* existence.

Please don't follow any healing advice in this book. I write books, I don't heal people… Although I have done my research, I'm not an expert.

If you want to find out more about healing, get in touch with www.ukhealers.info

The Witch Trials unveiled some of the most horrific crimes against innocent women ever seen in this country. A petition to pardon them received 13,157 signatures in January 2024. This response was received.

'The Government acknowledges the historic injustices of people accused of witchcraft between the 16th and 18th centuries. However, there are no plans to legislate to pardon those who were convicted.'

The word Wicce in the form I've used throughout the book, has nothing to do with the Wiccan religion but, as shown on the front pages of this book, is an early word for Witch. It also meant Wise Woman - a fitting description.

Disclaimer

This is a work of fiction and any resemblance between people, places and events is entirely coincidental. Any of the views held by the characters are not necessarily my own.

Printed in Great Britain
by Amazon